Hair of the Dog

An Arrow Investigations Action-Adventure Mystery

KC Walker

Acknowledgments

Mariah Sinclair designed my stunning and delightful cover. You can find her at https://www.thecovervault.com.

Thank you to Alyssa Lynn Palmer for your copy-editing expertise.

Special thanks to the 1667 Club for the sprints, the laughs, the plot parties, and the moral support. You guys mean the world to me.

Last, but never least, a super big dose of gratitude to my readers. You give me inspiration, ideas, and encouragement—and find the most persistent of typos! You are what makes all the hard work worthwhile.

Chapter One

I burst into the kitchen, my blanket clutched around my shoulders like a cape. "It's snowing!"

"Good morning, Whitley," my grandmother Bobbie said with a chuckle. "It snows every winter, though it is a bit early this year. Just a light dusting, really."

I hurried to the window and pushed the cafe curtains to one side. Mother Nature had sifted a layer of powdered sugar over the neighborhood—roofs, trees, and cars were hidden under a layer of clean, white fluff. If the snow didn't all melt, I might have my first white Christmas.

Bobbie, still dressed in her robe and slippers, poured me a cup of coffee. "Sit down. I have something to tell you."

Nothing good ever started with, "I have something to tell you."

Taking a seat across from her, I wrapped my hands around the warm mug and held my breath. "What is it?"

"You remember the mix-up about Kit's microchip? How Kit's previous owner reported her stolen?"

At the mention of her name, Kit, our rescue Chihuahua-and-who-knew-what-else, came bounding down the hall, greeting me with an excited yip. She tugged on my sock and gave it a nibble.

I reached down and gave her ears a scratch. "You said you and Bernard were taking care of things."

Bernard Fernsby, the grizzled private investigator who'd agreed to take Bobbie on as his apprentice, had decades of experience on and off the police force. At that moment, I questioned his competence.

"We're still working on it," Bobbie said. "The owner is being unreasonable."

"And you're just now telling me?"

Bobbie took a long sip of coffee before answering. "I didn't want to worry you unnecessarily."

Kit jumped on my lap and lay her head on my shoulder. Holding her close, I did my best to organize my thoughts and make a plan. I'd never wanted a dog, but now that I'd gotten attached to the little rascal, I wasn't about to let anyone take her from me.

"We'll leave town," I blurted out. "We'll go from place to place, never setting down roots, not giving anyone our real names. I'll get a burner phone and call you once a month to let you know we're okay."

Bobbie folded her arms over her chest and narrowed her eyes. "That's a little dramatic, don't you think?"

"What am I supposed to do?" My voice turned shrill, but I didn't care. "Just sit here and wait for them to come back and take her away from us? We don't know what kind of person this Jonathan What's-His-Name is."

"Jonathan Vance. Turns out he's a dog trainer in Riverside. His dogs perform for state fairs and special events, and he hires them out for movies and events, from what I gather."

Kit pawed my shoulder, trying to get my attention. She gave me puppy dog eyes, like a child who got caught keeping a secret. "That's where she learned all those tricks?"

"I suppose so. Although it doesn't explain how she can jump three times her height. She's an unusually nimble dog."

"Why didn't you talk to this Jonathan Vance guy and make some kind of deal?"

"We tried," Bobbie said, hanging her head in defeat. "His daughter handles the business end of things, and she's very stubborn. She insisted they wouldn't give Roxy up for any amount of money."

"Roxy?" Now I felt lost. "Who's that?"

"They called her Foxy Roxy because she looks like a little fox."

I mimicked throwing up. "Please never call her that again."

"What? Foxy Roxy?" Bobbie spoke to Kit in a singsong voice. "Is your name Roxy?"

Kit jerked her head in Bobbie's direction and a low growl came from somewhere deep inside her little body.

"I don't think Kit likes that name," I said. "And I'd really like to know why she feels so strongly about it."

"We can ask Mr. Vance when we meet with him tomorrow," Bobbie said.

"Huh? Are we driving to Riverside in the morning?"

"No, no," Bobbie shook her head. "Mr. Vance is coming into town sometime later today and spending the night at the Arrow Springs Inn. He's asked us to turn over Kit to him in the morning."

I slumped in my chair, planning to spend the day sulking.

"We'll work it out, Whit." Bobbie patted my hand reassuringly. "There's nothing for you to worry about."

"Promise?"

"I promise." Her warm smile reassured me. "You know what? You should get out today, maybe go into town. Or are you planning to hibernate until spring?"

"I tended bar at Gypsy's the other night." Gypsy's Tavern, a local watering hole with a limited menu, had been my only source of income since my last stunt job ended several months earlier. I'd begun to worry that I'd been blacklisted after a run-in with a director.

Bobbie refilled her own mug and sat back down. "That's the only time you've ventured out all week."

I checked the weather app on my phone. "It was fifty degrees yesterday, but today it says the high is only twenty-three. Is that possible?" In Los Angeles, where I'd spent most of my life, it was no doubt warm and sunny.

Bobbie chuckled, leading me to believe it was not only possible, but probable. It seemed wise to stay indoors, but I'd developed a serious case of cabin fever.

I carried my empty mug to the sink. "I suppose it wouldn't hurt to get some fresh air. Maybe I'll head into town—hit the gym and bring us back some pastries." The local coffee shop made cinnamon rolls the size of your head with enough icing to induce a sugar coma.

"Sounds great." Bobbie wrapped both hands around her warm mug. "I hope you're not planning to drive."

I narrowed my eyes at her. "Why not?"

"Allow me to explain the logistics of living in the mountains," she began, sounding smug about delivering an early-morning lecture. "Until they salt the roads, it's not safe to drive."

I pulled the blanket closer around me. "But it's cold out there."

"You've got that nice warm parka Angela got you, and you'll warm up in no time once you get the blood flowing."

My uncle and his wife, Angela, had adopted me as an infant when my birth mother left me behind and moved back to South America, where she'd lived for several years. My relationship with my parents was complicated, to say the least. But Angela did get me a very warm, and very red parka, so there was that.

"Just be careful going down the steep part of the road."

"I'll have you know I'm perfectly good at walking," I quipped. "I've had years of experience."

Bobbie gave me a smug smile. "Great, then you can take Kit out for her morning walk."

At the sound of the word "walk," Kit jumped off my lap and began prancing in circles.

"If I take her with me, I won't be able to go to the gym." As much as I appreciated an excuse to skip my workout, I'd already missed several days, and I needed to be ready when I got called for a job—whenever that might happen. As often as I reminded myself that little hiring happened over the holidays, I clung to a thin thread of hope.

Bobbie took another long sip of her coffee, obviously plotting some scheme or another. She gave me one of her sweetest smiles. "I'll take Kit for her morning walk if you run some errands for me."

Twenty minutes later, I stepped out the front door bundled up in my coat, scarf, gloves, and hat. I tucked Bobbie's long list of errands in my pocket and set off. The road curved and dipped toward town, and I soon found out Bobbie was right—I felt warmer already.

The street had been plowed and salted, and I grumbled, "Darn it. I could have driven." I found it hard to stay mad at Bobbie as I took in the enchanting scene surrounding me. A thin blanket of pristine snow covered every inch of the ground and icicles hung from eaves like crystalline chandeliers. Each breath I took filled my lungs with crisp, clean air scented with a hint of pine needles.

The road dipped sharply, and before I knew it, my foot slipped out from under me. I fell on my backside and slid down the road, flailing my arms in a futile attempt to grab on to something. As I picked up speed heading toward the intersection, I thought, "Is this how it all ends?" and "I hope no one is filming."

At the bottom of the hill, I squeezed my eyes tightly as I plowed into a huge snowbank at the side of the road. Stunned, I took stock of all my body parts, wiggling my fingers and toes. Relieved that everything appeared to be working normally, I sat up and shook the snow out of my hair. Where had my hat gone? As I attempted to get my feet, I heard a slow clapping sound.

Wouldn't you know it? Elijah, the hot bartender from Gypsy's Tavern and my occasional coworker, stood nearby with a huge grin on his face. A few passersby watched with wide eyes.

"Looking for this?" He held out my hat, waving it at me.

"A little help would be nice," I grumbled. "That is, if you're done applauding my latest stunt."

Elijah strolled over to me and reached out a hand to help me up. "I suppose an encore is out of the question."

I stood and snatched the hat from him then began brushing the snow from my jeans.

"Would you like some help with that?" His tone was definitely flirtatious, which I found encouraging after just making a fool of myself.

"Thanks, I can manage." I glared at five or six people still gawking. "Show's over folks. Move along."

Doing my best to act like nothing had happened, I headed for the gym. Elijah walked alongside me.

"I'm glad I ran into you," he said. "I have a party to go to on Christmas Eve, and I wondered..."

He hesitated, and I waited expectantly. Was he finally going to ask me out on a date?

"Gypsy won't give me the evening off unless I find someone to cover for me. Whattaya say? You'd really be helping me out."

I felt the last of my dignity leave my body. "I'm pretty sure I have plans," I lied, "but I'll double check and get back to you."

Elijah and I parted ways. I walked past the General Store and the laundromat, finally arriving at the gym. As I pushed the door open, I felt something brush against my leg.

The hunky guy with enormous arms at the reception desk greeted me with, "You can't bring your dog in here."

I looked down at my feet, and sure enough, there stood Kit, batting her big brown eyes at me.

"Why can't I bring my dog in here?"

That question stumped him for a moment. "Because it's against the rules." He pointed to a sign on the front door.

Thinking fast, I said, "But she's my emotional support dog. And I really, really need to work out. I'll be going back to work after the first of the year, and they'll expect me to be in fighting form. You know I'm a stunt performer, right? Mostly TV. I'm practically famous."

He blinked but otherwise didn't move, not even a twitch.

"She's very well behaved." I pointed at Kit and said, "Sit." She laid down. "We're working on that, but she won't make a peep, I promise."

The door opened and Kit began barking furiously at the man who entered. I sighed. "You're cramping my style, you know that, girl?"

Practicing the one trick we'd perfected, I patted my chest and said, "Alley-pop!" She leapt into my arms and gave my chin a lick.

I carried her outside so we could have a conversation without prying ears listening. "Listen, Kit. You can't keep sneaking out of the house. One day, it's going to get one of us in trouble. And with my luck, it'll be me."

With Kit tucked under one arm, I pulled Bobbie's list out of my pocket. I resisted the urge to go straight to the bakery for cinnamon rolls and instead headed for the General Store.

A young woman with a perky ponytail pushed a stroller along the wooden sidewalk. She smiled hesitantly when she saw me, possibly not having yet forgiven me for accusing her of murder over Thanksgiving weekend.

"Hey, Jenna." I plastered a friendly expression on my face as I got closer. "You and Mr. Whiskers out for a stroll?"

A mewing sound came from the stroller, and Jenna pushed the shade back, revealing a black and white tuxedo cat. "He still misses Martha, I think." She blinked back sympathetic tears. "But I think he'd adjusting. He does like our little walks."

"He's lucky to have you." Hoping to avoid a lengthy conversation, I gave her a wave and made a beeline for my next destination.

Walking through the doors of the General Store felt like stepping back in time. With no big box store within at least fifty miles, the store held nearly every category of product a shopper might want, all at exorbitant prices.

Scooter's mouth dropped open when I entered, possibly because he'd had a crush on me since we were kids, though it could have been because of the dog under my arm. He blushed, unable to speak, so I gave him a nod and headed for the back of the store. I passed by a dusty display of discounted items left over from Halloween and Thanksgiving, sorry to see all the candy had sold out.

"I should have grabbed a basket," I mumbled as I tucked a quart of milk under my dog-free arm and carried a dozen eggs to the front counter. Adding a pack of beef jerky from the display, I reached for my wallet.

Scooter mumbled something as he rang me up.

"Sorry, what did you say?" I asked.

He took a deep breath, as if steeling up his nerve. "No dogs allowed in the store."

"Oh, gotcha. I'll make sure to remember that. Thanks."

I carried my bag of groceries out and stood in front of the store, taking another look at Bobbie's errand list. Across the street, the imposing granite edifice that was the Arrow Springs Inn looked cozy with a layer of snow on the roof and icicles hanging from the edge of the roof. A lit Christmas tree twinkled in the window. If Kit weren't with me, I could hop on in for a nice, warm cup of cocoa—with extra marshmallows, of course.

A woman bundled up against the cold headed for the inn's front door. I caught her profile as she glanced over her shoulder and a jolt went through my body. I knew that face.

Julia, my birth mother.

Chapter Two

I froze in place, wondering if my vivid imagination had gotten the better of me. I'd never seen Julia in person—only in pictures. Surely, she would have let me know she was in town, or Bobbie would. Or would she?

Time to find out.

As I stepped off the curb, a car horn honked. Kit, startled by the sound, slipped out of my arms and took off running, her long, fluffy tail flying behind her. With one longing look at the inn, I took off after my wayward dog.

"I'm going to get you for this," I huffed as I chased after her.

A few blocks down the street, Kit stopped to sniff a clump of grass, one of her favorite activities.

"Hey girl." I slowed down to a trot. "Want a treat?"

At the word treat, her ears came to attention and her eyes locked with mine. I dug in the shopping bag for the jerky and broke off a small piece. "Here you go."

Before she knew what I was doing, I snatched her up. "Ha ha, I've got you." As I headed back to the inn, we had a heart-to-heart talk. "I really don't appreciate your attitude, missy, running off like that."

Kit blinked her big brown eyes at me, nearly melting my reserve.

"I'm serious," I scolded. "No more treats for you."

As I walked along the sidewalk, keeping an eye out for icy patches, I had an eerie feeling someone was watching me. Glancing over my shoulder, I observed the few people who'd ventured outside. No one looked familiar or suspicious.

I pulled open the inn's heavy, carved wooden door and stepped into the sauna-like interior. Switching Kit from one arm to the other so I could take my parka off, I surveyed the lobby, decorated for the season with a towering Christmas tree by the front window. An immense stone fireplace to my left, with flames dancing and crackling, explained why it felt so warm. The mantel, covered in greenery and red ribbons, twinkled with tiny white lights.

At the far end of the room, a carpeted staircase with intricately carved handrails led to the second floor, and past that, a sign for the dining room announced they were serving breakfast.

Dark, polished wood furniture had been arranged in conversation groupings. My gaze stopped at each person in the room—a flannel-clad couple reading by the fire, a silver-haired woman at a table by the window with a mug of coffee, and a younger woman with spiky pink hair scrolling on her phone. No one bore any resemblance to Julia.

I turned my attention to the check-in desk. A dapper, middle-aged man in a three-piece suit made eye contact, raising one questioning eyebrow. He wore his hair cropped short and his gray-streaked beard neatly trimmed. I headed over to talk with him.

"Checking in?"

Glancing at his name tag, I said, "Just looking for someone, Gary." Not sure how much I wanted to divulge to this stranger, I forged ahead, telling him as little as possible. "I saw a woman I recognized come in here. I'm almost sure it's... an old friend of mine I haven't seen for years. Reddish brown, shoulder length hair. Around fifty?"

"Doesn't ring any bells."

I wasn't about to give up that easily. "She's quite beautiful. I'm sure you would have noticed her." If he was faking his blank stare, he was doing a great job of it. "Her name is Julia."

Still no reaction other than an unconvincing customer service smile. "I'm sure you know we can't share any information about our guests."

"Oh, sure. Of course not." I considered my limited options. I could hardly go up and down the halls knocking on doors. If Julia had a room at the inn, that's probably where she'd be, but I figured I should check the dining room to be thorough.

Gary watched me impatiently. "Will there be anything else?"

"Huh?" I refocused my attention on him. "How's the food at your restaurant?"

He brightened up at the question. "The breakfast buffet is quite good. I highly recommend the Belgian waffles and apple smoked bacon. However, I'm afraid dogs aren't allowed in the dining room."

"Thanks. I'll just take a quick peek and come back another time without her."

Before he could object, I headed for the dining room. A server in a shirt and vest headed my way, but I held up one finger to hold her off. After scanning the room and not seeing anyone who remotely resembled Julia, I turned to go, running smack into a tall, cashmere sweater wearing hunk of man straight out of GQ.

"Sorry." I grimaced, while Kit's wagging tail whacked against my ribs.

He chuckled. "My fault entirely. Hey, aren't you Whit, the bartender at... what's the name of that place?"

"Gypsy's Tavern. I help out from time to time. I'm a stunt performer in my real job."

"Like for the movies?"

"Yeah, but mostly TV." I gazed into amber eyes trimmed with long, dark eyelashes, not sure if I felt mesmerized or jealous. Before he got the wrong idea, or the right idea, I shrugged. "Well, I guess I'll see you around."

"Have you had breakfast? Want to join me?"

I gestured to the remarkably well-behaved dog under my arm. "Can't. Dog."

"Oh, right. She sure sheds a lot, doesn't she?" He reached out and plucked a hair from my jacket. "Well, maybe I'll see you again at Gypsy's Tavern. I'm Henry, by the way."

"I'm Whit," I said before I could stop myself. "But you already knew that, so… see you later. Maybe."

I made my way back through the lobby, tugging my coat on as I went. I stood by the front door, hoping Julia might somehow appear so I could ask all the questions I'd been saving up my whole life.

Stepping outside, I took a few steps and turned back. "Where are you, Julia?" I whispered. "Are you here in Arrow Springs or just a figment of my imagination?"

I became aware Kit and I were the only creatures out on the sidewalk. Everyone with any sense stayed indoors or had found a warm spot to spend the day. What did that say about me?

❖ ⇒ ❖

When I stepped inside Sugarbuns Bakery, I breathed in the aromas of cinnamon, vanilla, and the yeasty smell of bread dough rising. The rosy-cheeked young woman behind the counter didn't blink an eye when I entered with Kit under one arm. Her short, honey-colored hair flipped at the ends in a way I found annoying when my hair did it. On her it looked effortlessly stylish.

She leaned over the counter and grinned at my dog. "What a cute little thing you are," she cooed. "Yes, you are, and you know it, don't you?"

Kit squirmed in my arms, basking in the attention. Why did my little runt of a dog reduce grown adults to baby-talking fools?

The baker lady came around from behind the counter, reaching out her arms.

"She's gonna—" I began, but my warning wasn't fast enough. Kit lunged straight into the woman's arms.

"Wow! Aren't you a talented little thing?" As she snuggled Kit closer, she got several chin licks. "Did you train her?"

I considered taking credit, but since it was almost Christmas and Santa might still consider putting me on his "good girl" list, I told her the truth. "She came that way. She even does a back flip."

"Wow, that's cool. My boyfriend won't let me have a pet. He says he's allergic, but I think he just doesn't like getting fur all over the sofa and everything."

Her polo shirt was now covered in light brown dog hair, so I could see his point.

When she finally handed Kit back, I perused the pastry case, just in case they'd come up with a new zero calorie treat to delight the taste buds. They hadn't, so I ordered three cinnamon rolls—one for Bobbie, one for me, and one backup for emergencies.

She handed me the bag. "Bring her back to see me so I can get some more doggy snuggles, okay?"

The door opened and a middle-aged blonde woman entered, pulling off her mittens. She gave me and Kit the side eye, which told me it was time to leave before we got the nice baker lady in trouble.

With a wave goodbye to Kit's new best friend, I carried my dog and the bag outside and headed up the hill to the house. My arm ached carrying the five-pound dog, a signal I needed more gym time.

Switching Kit to my other arm, I grumbled, "If I could only trust you, I wouldn't have to carry you."

At the top of the hill, I slowed my pace. What was I going to say to Bobbie? If she knew Julia was in town, why didn't she tell me? I couldn't think of a reason that Julia would visit Arrow Springs and not tell Bobbie, but it really stung to think she'd be so close and not want to see me.

I stood on the doorstep, unsure of how to approach the subject with my grandmother. Stepping inside, the scent of the Douglas fir Christmas tree, along with at least a dozen scented candles, nearly made me gag.

Holidays growing up had taught me to expect disappointment. Oh sure, there were presents under the tree—just not the ones I'd asked for. My parents dressed me in stiff, scratchy clothes for holiday gatherings where I was expected to be the perfect child, seen but not heard. This year, with Bobbie, things would be different. I just knew it.

After putting the milk and eggs in the fridge, I called out Bobbie's name. She answered from the space she called her crafting room. Kit followed me down the hall and bounded into the room when I pushed the door open.

Bobbie looked up from the computer just in time for Kit to jump on her lap. I made my way around the craft table where a half-finished collage lay forgotten.

She typed a few more words on an email, hit send, then turned her chair toward me. "You're back sooner than I expected."

"Kit got out again." I perched on the edge of the sewing cabinet. "They wouldn't let me work out at the gym with her, so I got your groceries and came back."

"Thank you, dear." She returned her attention to the computer monitor.

"While I was out, I walked by the Arrow Springs Inn,"

I began, intending to broach the subject of my birth mother carefully. "I could have sworn I saw Julia going in. Do you know anything about that?"

Bobbie stopped typing. "What are you talking about?" She appeared genuinely surprised. "Would you even recognize her? You haven't seen her since you were an infant."

"I've seen pictures. And besides the superficial resemblance, there was something familiar about her. I can't put my finger on it, but I think it was the way she moved, sort of like I do. Cat-like."

Bobbie nodded thoughtfully. "Do you call it 'cat-like' the way you slid down the road on your behind?"

How she'd already heard about my misadventure wasn't important. She might find the subject uncomfortable, but I wasn't going to let her distract me.

"Bobbie." I waited until I was sure I had her full attention. "I'm going to ask you directly and I'd like a straight answer." Sucking in a breath to steel myself, I asked, "Is Julia in town?"

Bobbie's eyelashes fluttered. Was she thrown off by my question or buying time to think of a response? "I honestly have no idea where Julia is."

Whenever someone used the word "honestly" I assumed they were lying. Otherwise, why did they need to say it? I didn't like to think that Bobbie would lie to me, especially about something so important.

"I haven't heard from her in months. She sent me that picture that's on the mantel the previous August but didn't tell where she was and didn't give me any way to contact her. Not even an email address."

"No note?"

"There was a personal message. For me."

"What was the message?"

"It was personal."

I felt my spine stiffen as my anger rose to the surface, but I held it at bay. "What was the message?" I repeated slowly.

Bobbie slumped in her chair. Kit nuzzled her arm as if sensing her distress.

I felt for her too, but this was my birth mother we were talking about. My parents had told me so little about Julia, and I knew it was a painful subject for Bobbie. After all, Julia was her only daughter, and who knew when she'd last seen her. I'd never pushed Bobbie for more information until now.

Bobbie's voice, normally so strong, quavered. "The message said, 'I still haven't forgiven you.'"

I repeated the words in my head. *I still haven't forgiven you.* "For what?"

We stared at each other for several seconds before she spoke. "She didn't say, but she didn't have to. She'll never forgive me for convincing her to give you up."

Bobbie's words hit me like a piano dropped from a tenth-floor window, and I struggled to catch my breath. I squeezed my fists tightly, feeling my nails dig into my palms.

"I've accepted that," Bobbie said, her voice more confident. "I still think—no, I know it was for the best. Especially for you."

"How do you know what's best for me?" I stood, not sure if I wanted to run to my room or stay and confront my grandmother.

"Julia made the choice. Not me. It wasn't safe for you as long as she stayed with him."

"Him who?" I asked. "My birth father? You don't think he would have been good to me?"

"It's not your father I worried about."

"Then who?"

"Your grandfather."

"Gramps?" Bobbie's husband, the best grandpa ever, had passed away several years ago. Why would she have worried about him?

"No. Your father's father."

I'd never given much thought to the obvious fact that I had another set of grandparents out there somewhere. "Julia wouldn't allow him to hurt me." After all, she was my mother. Didn't mothers protect their children at all costs?

Bobbie rocked back and forth, clearly disturbed by our conversation. It was a side of her I'd never seen before, and I didn't like it. She was my rock.

"Why won't you talk to me about her?" Walking over to the treadmill, I began digging it out from yards of fabric draped over it. I wanted to punch something, like the wall, but instead I flipped the switch, and the machine whirred to life. "I deserve the truth."

"The truth isn't all it's cracked up to be."

"Fine. But I'm not letting it drop this time. I won't rest until I find out the whole story." Where could I find someone who knew what had really happened? If not from the people I called mom and dad and not from

Bobbie, then who? There was only one person left to ask. Julia.

⟡ ⟶⟞

Bobbie left me alone to run off my frustrations. I'd gone three miles according to the treadmill's display when there was a knock on the front door.

"Helloooo!" a voice called out.

I turned off the treadmill and headed into the living room.

Bobbie and Kit reached the door before me. "Hurry on in, Rosa, before all the warm air gets out."

"I'm coming, I'm coming." Seventy-something Rosa, her dark hair slicked back into a low bun, spoke with a slight Mexican accent.

"How's your wrist?" I first met Rosa when she'd taken a tumble down her back steps. Bobbie was the only one who'd believed it was sabotage, and she'd ended up being right.

"It's much better, thanks," She pulled off her hat, gloves, and three or four layers of coats and sweaters, handing everything to Bobbie.

Bobbie hung up the last of Rosa's sweaters. "Have a seat in front of the fire. I'll make a pot of tea and fill you both in."

"I got cinnamon rolls," I said. "There's one for you too."

"That sounds lovely." Rosa set her oversized purse on the coffee table with a clunk.

Bobbie looked at her suspiciously. "What have you got in there?"

Rosa didn't answer right away, busying herself with settling onto the sofa. Finally, she gave Bobbie and me a sheepish look. "I need protection. There've been two murders in town just this year. People I actually know. Not to mention the attack on me."

"Bobbie and I put the bad guys behind bars," I said. With a little help from the police, that was, when they finally believed us.

Rosa watched as Bobbie lifted her purse and set it back down. "But now Bobbie says a stranger has come to town to take Kit away. Who knows what might happen?"

"I'm going to ask you one more time," Bobbie said. "What's in there?" When Rosa didn't answer, Bobbie brazenly opened the clasp and looked inside.

Her eyes widened. "A gun?" She pulled it out of the bag with two fingers and set it on the table. "Is that even registered?"

I inspected what appeared to be an antique pistol. "How old is that thing?"

"My late husband brought it back from the war as a souvenir," Rosa explained. "I think it's German."

Bobbie pulled out a few more items from Rosa's purse, listing them off one by one. "Pepper spray, smoke bomb, taser." Her mouth dropped open as she held up an object I recognized. "Is that a ninja star?"

"It's called a shuriken," I said. "That looks like a manhi shuriken. You can tell because the corners hook outwards. It makes them easier to grip and they do more damage. A win-win in my book."

Rosa grinned. "I bought a few of them online and they just arrived the other day. I haven't been able to practice with them yet, but I watched some videos, and it doesn't look that hard."

"I can teach you if you want. It's been a while, but I used to be pretty good at throwing them." I picked up the shuriken and aimed at the wall.

Bobbie waved her hands frantically. "Don't you dare throw that thing in the house."

Bobbie held out the pepper spray and put it back in the purse. "You can keep this. The rest I'm holding onto for safe keeping." It took two trips for her to carry the items into the kitchen.

Rosa scowled and turned to me. "Next thing Bobbie's going to want to take away my snowmobile."

Bobbie overheard her. "Of course I'm not going to take it away, but I am going to insist that you get your eyes checked before you go riding it around town. Last winter, you ended up in a ditch."

"That wasn't my fault," Rosa protested. "When there's that much fresh snow, it's hard to tell where the edge of the road is. Besides, no one was hurt."

"That time."

Rosa pouted until I brought out the cinnamon rolls. By the third bite, she seemed to have forgotten all about her arsenal. Of course, for all we knew, she had more weapons at home.

"I'm going to finish my workout," I announced. After that cinnamon roll, I had about another thousand calories to burn off. Running on the treadmill bored me to tears, but it was better than no exercise at all.

"That's good, dear," Bobbie said, and Rosa grinned. They seemed a little too happy to have me leave the room, which I found concerning.

What were they up to this time?

Chapter Three

When I finished another five miles on the treadmill followed by a quick shower and change of clothes, I found Gypsy had arrived, joining Bobbie and Rosa eating lunch at the kitchen table.

Gypsy, with her gray-streaked, long, wavy hair, looked like the free-spirited, bohemian woman her name implied, and her personality matched. I'd known her since I was a child when Bobbie and Gramps would take me into Gypsy's Tavern for dinner without telling Angela.

"Hey, Whit." Gypsy raised one of her painted-on eyebrows. "Maybe you can help."

"Depends." I liked to know what I was volunteering for before I committed myself.

"I've decided to change my name, and I'm looking for suggestions."

"You're not going to be Gypsy anymore?" I asked. "What about Gypsy's Tavern?" I'd grown up going to her restaurant, and I wasn't sure I liked the idea of a name change.

Her eyebrows tightened. "That has to change, too. I've learned that it's considered a slur, and I don't want my name to be offensive. I don't care if someone calls me woke —I've given it a lot of thought and I'm changing it."

Rosa spoke up. "I still don't see why. We don't have any Romani people living here. And besides, Gypsy's Tavern is practically an institution in Arrow Springs."

"And sometimes institutions have to change." Gypsy turned to me. "I'm thinking of Blythe. Or Gwendolyn. What do you think?"

"I suggested Windy, with an 'i'," Bobbie said, "but it didn't make the short list."

"Won't it be a pain to change your name?" I could only imagine the paperwork that might be involved. "You'll have to change your driver's license, social security card, your Tinder profile..."

"How did you know—?" Gypsy blushed and reached into her purse hanging over the back of her chair. She pulled out her wallet and showed me her license.

"Karen?" I laughed. "You're a Karen?"

She glared at me. "I'm not 'a Karen,' and stop calling people that. It's insulting to the million or so women named Karen."

"Sorry." Apparently, I'd hit a touchy subject. "You never changed your name legally to Gypsy?" I took another look at the license. "Your middle name is Sunshine?"

"It is?" Bobbie snatched the license out of my hand and looked for herself. "It is! How did I never know that?"

Gypsy rolled her eyes. "I'm a sixties baby. My mom was a hippie, but my dad insisted I get a respectable first name."

"Sunshine is perfect for you," Bobbie said.

Since Gypsy didn't seem convinced, I added, "or Sunny for short."

Rosa finally spoke up. "You *are* a ray of sunshine to everyone you meet. I think it's the perfect name for you."

Bobbie handed back Gypsy's license. "I agree."

"Sunshine." A smile formed on Gypsy's lips. "Sunny." She nodded. "I'll need to think about it a bit more, but it's starting to grow on me."

"And you can call your place Sunshine Tavern," Bobbie suggested.

"I'll have to check trademarks and all that, but I do like the sound of that."

"Great," I said. "It's settled." I held out a hand. "Nice to meet you, Sunny." That would take some getting used to. "Don't get mad at me if I call you the wrong name, okay?"

"No problem," she said. "Old habits are hard to break."

❖ ❖

After an afternoon scrolling social media, I questioned whether I'd survive a winter in Arrow Springs with so little to do. I emerged from my room and found Bobbie by herself in the kitchen, browsing through a cookbook.

While Bobbie picked out a recipe for dinner, I quietly made my way to the fireplace and scanned the collection of framed photos arranged on the mantel until I found the latest picture of Julia. My heart raced with anticipation as I removed the photo from its frame and slipped it into my pocket. I replaced the frame on the mantel, wondering how long before Bobbie noticed the missing photo.

After our awkward conversation that morning, Bobbie seemed determined to pretend that nothing was wrong. That was okay with me for the time being.

I stuck my head in the kitchen. "I'm going to take a walk into town."

"I'm glad you're getting out more." She gave me the once over. "Don't forget your gloves and hat."

"And scarf. I know."

"And it will be getting dark soon. Take a flashlight."

"My phone has a flashlight," I reminded her.

Two motives sent me to the Arrow Springs Inn that evening. First, to talk to Mr. Jonathan Vance to see what kind of person he was and hopefully make a deal. Second, to find out if the woman I'd seen really was Julia.

My mother—Angela, not Julia—often said that anyone could be bought if you knew what they cared about most. Angela assumed most people wanted money, but I knew differently. Even those who craved money almost always wanted what it could bring—security, status, comfort, power... the list was endless.

If Kit's former owner hadn't been tempted by whatever terms Bobbie had suggested, then I had a feeling they wanted something other than money.

But what?

Once I was bundled up and ready to go, I returned to the kitchen. "Okay, see you."

Bobbie grinned. "You might want to see if the General Store carries cleats." She tilted her head to one side. "So you don't go sliding down the hill again."

"Ha ha," I said without humor. "How long until I live that down?"

"Would you take Kit with you?" Bobbie asked, her voice as sweet as honey. "I'm taking an online yoga class in about ten minutes, and you know how she climbs all over anyone who's on the floor."

Kit must have heard her name because she appeared out of nowhere. She'd probably been in her favorite hiding place, under the sofa.

"Just lock her in my room," I suggested.

"She'll howl until I let her out. It's hardly conducive to reaching a zen-like state of relaxation."

My shoulders tensed. I didn't want to take Kit with me to see Jonathan Vance, but I didn't want to tell Bobbie where I was going either. "I might stop in at Gypsy's Tavern for a drink. Can't take a dog to a restaurant."

Bobbie waved her hand in dismissal. "That's the way things are in big cities. Gypsy or Elijah won't mind."

"But it's cold out," I protested. "She'll freeze out there."

"Put on her booties and her new Christmas jacket. The one that makes her look like an elf. That'll make everyone smile."

I stared Bobbie down, hoping she'd give up on the idea, but she stared right back at me, her gaze steady. *Pick your battles,* an inner voice reminded me.

"Fine." I headed for the front door, Kit right on my heels. She cooperated while I put her jacket on, though she fought me on the boots. When I grabbed the leash, she began jumping three feet into the air.

"Sit," I commanded, so she lay down and rolled over on her back. I managed to attach the leash to her harness. It was like being stuck babysitting a younger sibling.

With us both bundled up against the elements, I stepped outside. Kit wagged her tail, excited to explore. I hoped any icy spots had melted during the day, but the road would be safer to walk on as long as I kept an eye out for cars.

"I'm not sure this is a good idea, Kit, but this might be my only chance to talk to this guy. You know, I've gotten used to having you around." My voice caught in my throat. I'd avoided attachments for the most part. If I didn't get close to anyone, I wouldn't get hurt.

Bobbie was the one exception. She didn't tell me I was rude or too blunt the way others often did. I got the feeling she knew I loved her, which I did—more than anyone else alive. And I knew she loved me.

And as for the little mutt at the end of my leash? She showed indiscriminate affection toward everyone, or at least the women she met. She seemed pickier about the men we ran into around town, but that seemed like a prudent approach to me.

Kit and I had a special bond and when she stared at me with her big, brown trusting eyes, I knew I couldn't let anyone take her away from us. I'd do whatever it took to keep her safe, and I got the feeling she knew it.

It took twice as long to get to our destination as it should have, since she had to sniff every bush, tree trunk, and signpost along the way. On top of that, everyone we passed had to stop us to compliment us on her holiday outfit. Kit wagged her tail and rubbed up against people's shoes.

As I approached the inn, I tucked Kit under my jacket. "Be quiet, okay? I don't want anyone to know you're with me."

As I stepped into the warm lobby, I regretted not being able to take my coat off. Kit squirmed in her warm hiding place, and I gave her a reassuring scratch behind her ear.

Gary, the gray-bearded man I'd seen earlier that day, stood behind the reception desk, and I deflated. No way would he give me Jonathan Vance's room number. I'd have to try the direct approach.

"I'd like to see one of your guests," I explained, giving him the name.

"Certainly." He didn't seem to recognize me, which was probably a good thing. "You may use the house phone to call and announce yourself." He pointed to a phone at the end of the counter.

I lifted the receiver, and the operator put me through. A man's voice answered.

"Mr. Vance, this is Whitley Leland. I'm in the lobby, and I wonder if you'd see me for a few minutes."

"Who?"

"Whitley Leland. I adopted Kit. I'd like to clear up the confusion about who she belongs to."

He harrumphed. "You mean Roxy. I can assure you there's no confusion. If you don't turn her over to me, I'm prepared to take further legal action."

This wasn't starting out well. "Can we just talk?"

After a long pause, he answered. "Fine. Room 281."

I walked across the thick carpet to a huge oak staircase and climbed to the second floor. At the end of a long hall, I found the room. Voices came from inside. Putting my ear close to the door, I tried to make out the words, but only muffled sounds came through. One voice, gruff and surly, definitely belonged to a man.

The other? I couldn't be sure, but I made out a few words. "That mutt's worth a lot. More than..." I couldn't decipher the rest of the sentence.

I knocked.

The door swung open to a scowling man in an untucked, dingy, beige polyester shirt. Only slightly taller than me and thick around the middle, he looked to be in his late forties or early fifties, with thinning hair and a double chin. He had one hand on the doorjamb and the other on the doorknob, as if making a barrier against entry. One chubby finger sported a thick gold ring with three diamonds. Or maybe they were cubic zirconium. It was hard to tell the difference.

"Mr. Vance?" I thought I should make sure I had the right room.

"Go ahead and say what you came to say." He belonged to the gruff and surly voice. "I'm not going to—"

Whatever he was going to say was interrupted by a growl coming from under my coat. I gave him a smirk and patted my stomach. "Indigestion."

He didn't buy it for a second. "You've got Roxy with you. Give her to me—she's my property..."

Did he just call Kit property?

Despite the anger I felt building inside me, I kept my voice steady. "Look, I came here to talk. She's happy with me and my grandmother. Doesn't that mean something to you?"

Before I knew it, Kit stuck her head out from under my coat. Vance reached for her but pulled his hand back when she bared her teeth. Kit's growl rose an octave, a sound I'd never heard before, something like a cheap weed whacker.

I couldn't help grinning. "I don't think she likes you very much."

"Hand her over." He reached for her, but she yipped and snapped at him like a hungry piranha.

Kit squirmed, and I struggled to keep from dropping her. Before I could stop her, she'd used her back legs to kick herself off from my ribs and landed on the carpet. Snarling, she nipped at his ankle then planted her teeth firmly onto his pant leg.

"Roxy! Let go, you horrible mutt!" He shook his leg, but she held on tightly, until he reached down to grab her.

Kit must have nipped him because he jerked his hand back, crying out, "You little—"

Before he could think of a name to call her, Kit took off running down the hall, and I ran after her. Her leash trailed as she dashed down the stairs to the front door.

"Kit! Stop!" I called after her, but she didn't slow down.

All faces turned to watch the little dog being chased through the lobby. The door opened as a woman entered, her hands full of colorful shopping bags.

"Don't let her out," I yelled, but it was too late. Kit slipped through the door, and I chased her down the street. She kept running, but I slowed down to a jog. I knew where she was going.

Home.

⋯ → ⋗

When I made it to Bobbie's house, Kit stood by the front door waiting for me. I didn't blame her for not wanting to sit and expose her backside to the cold porch.

"What's the matter?" I huffed. "Can't reach the door-knob?" That was one trick she hadn't yet learned.

Kit followed me inside and ran from room to room looking for Bobbie. When she found a closed door, she barked and snarled at it.

"Sorry if we cut your yoga short," I said when Bobbie came out of the den, Kit right on her heels.

"Why are you out of breath?" Bobbie asked.

"It's a long story."

"Did she get away from you again?" Her frown showed disappointment, though I wasn't sure if it was with me or Kit.

"I guess it's not that long of a story." I didn't want to share the rest of what had happened just yet.

Bobbie lit the gas fire and took a seat in front of it on the sofa. Kit jumped up and snuggled next to her, burrowing under the afghan.

The idea of snuggling under a blanket in front of a warm fire tempted me, but I had other plans. "I'm heading back into town for a bit."

"Going to see Elijah?"

Elijah would be working that night at Gypsy's Tavern,

or whatever his mom decided to call the place. I didn't want to lie, so I told a half-truth instead. "Cabin fever is getting the better of me."

"Have fun and say hi to Gypsy—or rather Sunny—if she's there. And ask her if she's coming over for Christmas eve."

"Will do. Don't wait up."

As I stepped onto the front porch, getting a drink at Gypsy's didn't sound like a bad idea. I might even run into Henry again. I'd nearly convinced myself to stay away from Vance, but since when did I play it safe?

My decision made, I made a beeline back to the inn. I'd tell Vance that I'd come back to apologize and check on him. My real motive for going back to see him was to find out why Kit hated him so much. As her former owner, that didn't reflect well on him. After I expressed my sympathy for Kit attacking him, I planned to use her dislike of him as leverage.

When I entered the inn, the reception desk was vacant, which meant I didn't have to announce myself and risk being turned away. Relaxing my shoulders and keeping my chin up to appear like I belonged there, I took the stairs two at a time.

At the end of the hall, I stood outside of room 281 and took a deep breath before knocking. The door, not fully latched, opened a few inches.

"Hello?" I knocked again, harder. "Mr. Vance?"

No reply.

"Anyone home?" I pushed the door open a few more inches. Through the opening, the room appeared charming, decorated in a rustic, country style—lots of cotton chintz. On the dresser lay a phone and wallet.

Why had Vance left his door unlocked and unlatched? Had he gone after us and hadn't gotten back yet? He might be at Bobbie's right now, bullying her into letting him have Kit. I calmed down slightly when I reminded myself that Kit could defend herself.

With an extended index finger, I gave the door a little shove and leaned in to get a better look. Nothing seemed out of place.

Except the shoe on the floor. Normally, I wouldn't find that unusual, but the shoe was on a foot attached to a leg.

Pushing the door fully open, I gasped.

Jonathan Vance lay on the floor in a pool of blood.

Chapter Four

I didn't like Jonathan Vance, but someone else must have *really* hated him.

When reality penetrated my brain, I rushed back to the top of the stairs and called down to the lobby, "Call the police. Call the paramedics." The few people in the nearly empty lobby turned their faces toward me, but no one moved. "Call 9-1-1," I added for good measure.

Gary, back at his post, came out from behind the front desk, his brow creased with worry. "What's going on?"

"What is wrong with you people?" I muttered, remembering that I had a phone in my pocket. After dialing 9-1-1, I waited for someone to answer while watching the clerk come up the stairs in slow motion. Was he hesitant to see what I'd just seen, or had time slowed?

As the operator came on the line, I returned to the doorway of room 281 and spewed all the information in a frantic rush.

"Take a breath and try to calm down," the woman's voice calmly advised.

"Easy for you to say."

"Yes, I know, but please try. Now, repeat what you said, only slower this time. You think someone is dead?"

I glanced inside the room at Vance and the widening blood stain spreading on the carpet.

"His name is Jonathan Vance. I'm pretty sure he's dead. Like really dead." I took one step closer. What did he have clutched in his right hand?

"Have you checked his vitals?"

"Huh?" I pulled my eyes away from his motionless body. "Like take his pulse?"

"That's a start."

Did I detect a note of sarcasm in her voice? Nah, that was probably me projecting. I took another step into the room. The lamp on the nightstand had been knocked over and the bedspread partially pulled off the bed.

I knelt next to Vance and set my phone on the floor, pressing the button for the speaker. As I reluctantly touched my fingertips to his left wrist, my eyes involuntarily followed the red stain on the carpet to its source—his neck. I'd seen enough of Bobbie's favorite crime shows to guess he'd severed his carotid artery. The object he clutched in his other hand looked like a cheap knockoff Swiss army knife.

Something was missing, but what? I checked both hands—the ring was gone. Was robbery the motive? Would a thief steal a ring but leave a wallet and phone behind?

At the sound of footsteps behind me, I jumped to my feet and spun around in one smooth motion, prepared to defend myself, but it was just Gary. He took one look at the body, shrieked, and fell into a heap on the floor. I hurried over and crouched down next to him.

Giving him a good shake, I said, "Snap out of it, Gary."

A faint voice came from my phone where I'd laid it. "What's going on?"

I raised my voice so the woman on the other end could hear me. "The desk clerk just passed out when he saw the dead body. It was probably all the blood that did it. Did I mention the blood?" I patted Gary's cheek. "Hey, wake up."

"Paramedics are on the way." Her voice maintained an air of detachment, which impressed me.

"Good. This guy is out cold. Do you still want me to check the dead guy's pulse?"

Muttering voices from the hall grew in volume. A crowd had gathered, watching me intently. One face caught my attention, and I jumped to my feet. "Julia?" The woman disappeared.

"Someone get some water or something for Gary," I said as I pushed through the growing crowd. Where had the woman gone? If it wasn't Julia, then why had she run away?

Torn between two opposing mysteries, both very personal, my responsible nature took over, perhaps a sign of newfound maturity. Pushing my way back into the room, I took control of the situation.

"Everyone out," I yelled to those who'd crept into the

room. I waved at them, yelling, "Out, out, out," and slammed the door.

In the bathroom, I found a glass wrapped in paper stating it had been sanitized for my protection. I filled it with tap water and hurried back to Gary. Before I could toss it on his face, he began blinking.

"Oh good, you're back." Slightly disappointed that I didn't get to douse him, I helped him to a seated position. "Drink some water and don't look at the dead guy, okay?"

"The what?"

Of course, he did just what I'd told him not to. He gasped and clutched his chest at the sight, but at least he wouldn't fall if he passed out again.

Pounding on the door, someone called out, "Paramedics."

"Come in," I called back before realizing the door had locked automatically when I slammed it. The two men entered with oversized bags over their shoulders. I stepped into the hall to let them work, and the guests gathered there peppered Gary and me with questions.

"What happened?"

"Is he dead?"

"Is there a maniac on the loose?"

With a scowl at the person who asked the last question, I said simply, "No comment," and headed for the stairs. Gary passed me by, hurrying down the stairs and resuming his post at the front desk.

At the sound of the front door opening, Gary looked up, along with everyone in the lobby. Two Arrow Springs police officers made a beeline to his desk, and he pointed straight at me. I couldn't hear what they said, but the officers came up the stairs and headed in my direction.

I recognized Deputy Wallenthorp from a previous encounter, but not the much younger woman in uniform who accompanied him.

One guest stopped the officers halfway up the stairs. "What's going on? Are we in danger?"

Wallenthorp spoke in a strong and official tone. "I suggest you return to your room until we have more information."

He gave me a questioning look, possibly wondering what I was doing at the scene of another murder.

I pointed down the hall. "Room 281. The victim's name is Jonathan Vance."

He nodded. "I'll speak with you later."

Cheerful Christmas music played as more guests gathered in the lobby, whispering in small groups. By now, nearly everyone in the hotel probably knew about the dead body. Heck, probably half the town did by now. A terrible thought popped into my head—Bobbie would kill me if she heard the news from someone else.

Taking a seat at the top of the staircase, I dialed Bobbie's number.

"What's up?" she asked.

"Well," I began. "I went to see Vance at the inn..."

She launched into a lecture. "You're so impulsive. Why did you go without telling me what you were doing?

Now we're on the defensive, and I don't know how we're going to keep him from taking Kit from us."

"Um... I don't think that's going to be a problem."

"It's not?" she replied with a note of optimism.

"No." I steeled myself for her reaction. "Jonathan Vance is dead."

After a long silence, I glanced at the phone, thinking we'd been disconnected.

"Bobbie? Did you hear me?"

"Yes, I heard you." She lowered her voice to just above a whisper. "Did you kill him?"

"What? How could you think that?"

"As a private eye, I've got to ask the hard questions and not make any assumptions."

"Sheesh, Bobbie. This isn't a game. A man is dead."

"I'm on my way."

Before I could tell her to stay put, she'd hung up. I stood up too quickly, feeling lightheaded, then sat back down, not sure what I should do.

Wallenthorp hadn't exactly told me not to leave, but what would he do if they came looking for me and I'd left? I could leave my number with Gary. But as much as I wanted to go home and snuggle up in front of the fire with a hot toddy and a warm dog, I forced myself to wait. I wanted to hear what the deputies had to say.

A few minutes later, the paramedics carried a stretcher past me and down the stairs, Vance's body now covered in a sheet.

I crept down the hall toward room 281, hoping to catch some of the deputies' conversation. As I approached, the door flung open, and I found myself face to face with Deputy Wallenthorp.

When I'd first met him, I figured him to be at least fifty, but now that I had a good look, I guessed his age closer to forty. He'd obviously spent too much time in the sun without a good moisturizing sunscreen.

"Oh good," I said with a sigh of relief. "I was just wondering how long I was going to have to wait."

His barrel chest heaved in frustration, though I'd barely said a word. Had I perfected the talent of annoying people merely by my presence? It wasn't much of a superpower, but combined with my ability to spot synthetic fibers from fifty feet away, it might come in handy someday.

"Come with me," the deputy ordered, and headed down the hall.

I followed him down the stairs to the front desk, where he asked if there was a private room he could use to interview witnesses.

Gary blinked rapidly, his lips pursed. "Well... I don't know... I just..."

"Dude," I interrupted his flustered rambling. "Don't you have an office?"

"What? Yes, well, there's an office... it's not my office... my manager..."

"That will do." Wallenthorp's tone was brisk and authoritative.

Gary's eyes widened, possibly wondering what he was going to tell his boss, but he pointed at a door behind him.

"Say," I asked. "Where were you earlier, before I found Vance's body?"

"I-I," he stammered. "I was helping a guest with their remote. They said it wasn't working."

Wallenthorp narrowed his eyes at me. "I'll ask the questions, if it's all right with you." He turned his attention to Gary. "I'll need the guest's name and room number."

The deputy and I entered the small, windowless office. The beige industrial carpeting bore no resemblance to the plush carpets in the rest of the inn. Scattered papers covered a cheap, wood-grained desk with a computer and phone.

Instead of taking a seat behind the desk, Wallenthorp motioned to a small table and two chairs squeezed into a corner. Once we sat down, he pulled a notepad out of his breast pocket.

"Name?" he asked.

"Whitley Leland." I spelled it for him to avoid having the name Whitney ending up in my permanent record. I loved my unique name, but sometimes I found it exhausting to always have to correct people.

"And your address?"

"Well, I'm staying with my grandmother for the time being. I don't know if you remember meeting her—Bobbie Leland? Her real name is Roberta, but everyone calls her Bobbie except my mother, Angela. It's just temporary. My residence, that is."

"And your permanent address?"

That question threw me, and for the first time, it occurred to me I was technically homeless. Which seemed ironic considering how many homes my parents owned.

"I'll just give you Bobbie's address. I'll be there until after New Year's, and then I'll be moving back to L.A."

After we got the mundane details out of the way, Wallenthorp asked me to give him my version of the events of the evening up to finding Vance's body.

"I came here around four this afternoon to talk to him about letting us keep Kit." When Wallenthorp raised his eyebrows, I clarified. "Kit is my dog. I have as much right to her as Vance. Don't they say possession is nine-tenths of the law?"

He tightened his lips into a smirk. "Not when property has been reported stolen."

"She's not property," I sniped. "She's a dog."

He ignored my outburst. "Go on. What happened when you came to talk to him?"

"I heard voices through the door. There was a man with him. That must be who killed him after I left."

"Stick to the facts, please. Did you see this other person you claim was in the room?"

"No." I bristled at his inference that I might have been lying or mistaken. "Vance wouldn't let me into the room. He stood in the doorway and didn't open the door all the way."

I filled him in on our conversation and Kit's reaction to Vance. "I chased Kit all the way home. It couldn't have been over thirty or forty-five minutes until I got back here."

"Why did you come back?"

"We weren't done talking."

"And what happened when you arrived the second time?"

45

"The door was ajar and when I pushed it open, I saw him lying on the floor. Dead."

He nodded. "And then what happened?"

"I freaked out. Maybe finding a dead body in a hotel room is a regular occurrence for you, but I ran back out and started yelling down to Gary to call someone. He's the front desk clerk, and he's absolutely no good in a crisis. Then I remembered I had a phone and called 9-1-1."

"At 7:03 P.M."

"If you say so."

"The dispatcher reported you refused to check vitals or perform CPR."

I straighten up in my chair, ready for a fight. "You saw the guy. What was the point?"

"No point at all, in my opinion, but as you said yourself, you don't see dead bodies on a regular basis. How did you know he couldn't be resuscitated?"

My mind flashed back to the moment I opened the door and saw Vance's body, and I closed my eyes tightly, as if to shut out the memory. It didn't work.

Not wanting to say it out loud, I opened my eyes and whispered, "There was so much blood."

Wallenthorp's tone changed to one of concern. "Can I get you some water?"

"Thanks, but I just want to get this over and go home." I shook off the dark thoughts swimming in my brain. "What was the question again?"

"What happened after you entered the room?"

"I was on the phone with the 9-1-1 operator who wanted me to take his vitals. When I knelt to take his pulse, I saw the wound on his neck. I'm guessing his carotid artery was severed."

"I'll wait for the coroner's official findings, but off the record, you're probably right."

"Vance had a knife in his hand."

"Yes, we didn't find a note, but it was most likely suicide."

"Suicide?" I couldn't believe what I was hearing. "How can you say it was suicide? Didn't you see the signs of a struggle? The lamp knocked over? The bedspread pulled halfway off the bed? Time's a wasting, Deputy. You need to find whoever was in the room with him. I bet you anything that's who murdered Vance."

A knock on the door interrupted my rant. Wallenthorp called out, "Come in."

Bobbie bustled in looking somewhat askew with Kit on a leash. She must have left home in a hurry, since she hadn't even bothered with a swipe of lipstick. Or perhaps my news of the dead body had thrown her off her routine.

"This is my grandmother, Bobbie Leland," I told the deputy, hoping he didn't remember his previous encounter with her.

Kit pulled on the leash, trying to get to me.

"Is this the dog whose ownership is in question?" the deputy asked.

Bobbie unclipped the leash, and Kit dashed over and hopped on my lap. "There's no question who she belongs with. Just look at these two."

Kit licked my chin, and I snuggled her close and gave the deputy a smile, hoping to show how much we belonged together.

Bobbie kept talking. "I find talking about the owner-ship of animals as if they're inanimate objects distasteful. They should have some say in where they live, don't you agree?"

"It doesn't matter what I think, Mrs. Leland," Wallen-thorp grumbled. "According to the law, that dog is prop-erty. In addition, that dog may have something to do with the occurrences in this inn this evening."

"That dog has a name—Kit." Bobbie folded her arms in front of her. "And by occurrences, I assume you're refer-ring to the fact that a murder took place?"

"I am. And since the deceased has a court order requiring that his property be returned to him, I'll have to take custody of the dog until its rightful owner can be determined."

"You're taking her?" I jumped to my feet, clutching Kit, and gave Bobbie a glare. "Why did you have to bring her?"

"You know she always gets out."

Wallenthorp reached out to take Kit from me. I took one step back.

"Where will Kit stay until this mess is figured out?" Bobbie asked.

"I think the police station is the best place since someone will be there all night." He gave Bobbie a sympa-thetic smile. "I'll see what I can do to get this straightened out in the morning."

"Aren't you a little busy with, oh, I don't know... a murder investigation?" I didn't even try to keep the sarcasm out of my voice.

Bobbie took Kit from me and held her out for the offi-cer. Kit bared her teeth, and a low growl escaped her.

"Perhaps it would be best if I use the leash."

"Suit yourself." Bobbie clipped the leash to Kit's harness and handed the strap to him.

Kit resisted, but her five-pound weight was no match for the deputy. She rolled over on her back and turned her big brown eyes to me as he dragged her across the carpet. My heart twisted as she let out a soft whimper.

Chapter Five

The next morning, before opening my eyes, I patted the comforter for a dog-sized lump. We'd had a few morning mishaps, and I'd learned to check for Kit before I got out of bed.

When she didn't come out from the folds, the memories of the previous evening came flooding back, including the sight of Vance's dead body.

And the even more horrible fact that Kit was being held at the police station. Others might disagree at my rating of the catastrophes, but I'd barely known Vance, and he didn't seem like someone the world would miss.

At that thought, I heard Bobbie's voice in my head. "Every life is valuable. No one is disposable."

Sometimes it seemed like Bobbie was my personal Jiminy Cricket, a conscience walking around on two legs reminding me of right or wrong. I didn't mind too much since it saved me the trouble.

Rubbing my eyes, I pulled on the jeans I'd left on the

floor the night before, along with a T-shirt. I found my hoodie hanging from a door handle and made my way down the hall to the kitchen.

I greeted Bobbie with a yawn.

"Oh, good. You're up." Bobbie handed me a travel mug. "Get your shoes on. We're going to the police station."

Since Bobbie had dropped off a bed, blanket, food, and treats for Kit the night before, I hoped we were going to bring her home, but Bobbie's determined scowl led me to believe otherwise.

I zipped up my boots and grabbed my parka. "What's the plan?"

"I spoke to my lawyer this morning," Bobbie began as she stepped outside.

"You're just now calling your lawyer?" I followed her out the door into an enchanted scene, the only sounds the rustling of snow falling from the trees and a few bird calls. "Wow. More snow."

"This is so unusual this early in the season." Bobbie stared down the road and didn't look happy. "I suppose we'll have to walk."

I took in the sight of my car, covered in a thick layer of snow. With a huff, I stomped over to it to brush the snow off the windshield with my parka-covered arm.

Bobbie tugged at my arm. "It's not that far."

I could tell by her tone of voice that she wasn't any happier about walking than I was.

"As I was saying, I called my lawyer this morning because things have changed. I don't see how there can be an ownership dispute when one of the claimants is dead."

"That's right." Hope sparked, but quickly faded. "Legal action could take days. Is Kit going to spend the whole time in jail?" The thought seemed ridiculous, but it also broke my heart. "Poor thing, all alone in a cold cell."

"I doubt she's in a cell, and she won't be alone. My lawyer called the Arrow Springs police chief and insisted that as long as they're holding her, one of us be allowed to be with her. He threatened to accuse them of animal cruelty if they didn't."

"Good for him." As we made our way down the hill, I thought about what she said. "Does that mean we're going to spend the weekend in jail?"

Two blocks past the Arrow Springs Inn, we turned down a side street. Like most businesses in town, it had the style of a log cabin, with a wide overhang held up by rough-hewn logs.

Pushing open one of the glass doors, I held it open for Bobbie. The interior was devoid of charm, the designers sticking with an institutional beige theme. A few vinyl-upholstered chairs lined one wall, and a large bulletin board covered with notices hung on another. I made a beeline for the window at one end of the room.

"Let me," Bobbie called out, and I turned to wait for her, but she took too long.

I banged on the glass. "Hey. Officers. Somebody. We're here to see our dog."

Bobbie tapped me on the shoulder and pointed to a button to the left of the window with a sign stating, "Push for Assistance."

"Fine," I grumbled and pushed the button.

A uniformed woman appeared at the window, and her voice squawked through the speaker. "May I help you?"

After I explained why we were there, she said "Oh, thank the lord," and buzzed us through a door. Six gray metal desks arranged in two rows took up most of the space. Plaques, framed certifications, and more bulletin boards covered the walls.

"I'm Deputy Tuttle," the deputy said. "Come with me."

We followed her through a door in the back of the room, then down the hall. She came to a door and knocked. Holding the door open, she gestured for us to enter. "Maybe you can get her to come down."

Her words made no sense until I stepped into the room and saw Kit on top of a tall bookcase.

"Hey, girl," I greeted her and held out my arms.

To everyone's surprise except mine, Kit leapt off the top of the bookcase right into my arms.

I snuggled her close to me. "Have you been causing trouble?"

The deputy sighed. "I tried to get her to come down for hours, then finally gave up. I put her bed up there, but she shoved it off. She acted like she was going to do the same with her water, so I put it back on the floor."

"You must be thirsty." I carried Kit over to the bowl and set her down. She drank greedily, then gobbled down her food.

I plopped on the ground cross-legged and leaned against the wall. Kit jumped on me and climbed up my body until she reached my shoulder.

"You're not a parrot, you silly girl," I said, laughing as she licked my ear.

"I've spent the night here with your dog," Tuttle said, "so I'm going to clock out and go home. Make yourself comfortable while you wait."

"Wait?" I jumped to my feet. "What are we waiting for? And for how long?"

Bobbie spoke up. "We'd like to speak with Deputy Wallenthorp right away, please."

"Fine." The deputy opened the door as a buzzing came from the front room. She led us back to the front room and showed us a desk where we could wait.

The buzzing sound started again—buzz buzz buzz.

A deputy at one of the other desks called out, "Can you get that, Tuttle?"

Her face reddened, and she snapped at him. "Would you give me a moment?" Stepping up to the window, she spoke into a microphone. "May I help you?"

"I'm here to see Deputy Wallenthorp," a woman's voice said. "I'm Mrs. Vance. Mrs. Jonathan Vance."

Twisting around to get a look at Mrs. Vance, I caught a glimpse through the window of a middle-aged woman. Her knit cap partially hid a bouffant hairstyle that had been out of style for decades.

"I see," Tuttle said gently, adding, "I'm very sorry for your loss."

Mrs. Vance ignored the condolences. "Is Deputy Wallenthorp here or not? I drove all the way up here from Riverside to claim my husband's belongings."

"Let me buzz you in."

Mrs. Vance came through the door. She'd dressed in

several layers, giving her a round, lumpy appearance. The top layer, a zippered fleece sweatshirt, was the kind made from recycled soda bottles.

I whispered to Bobbie. "She drove up the hill this morning? In this weather?"

"Maybe she put chains on her car," Bobbie whispered back.

"And is she wearing a wig?"

"Shh..." Bobbie said.

The woman stopped when she saw us and Kit. "You." Her thick eyebrows drew together as her eyes narrowed. "You're the thieves who stole our dog."

I held Kit close to my chest to protect her from the mean lady.

Bobbie looked from the woman to Kit and back again. "Oh, really?" Bobbie reached out to take Kit from me, but I held her more tightly. Under her breath so that only I could hear, she said, "Trust me."

Bobbie took Kit from me and set her on the ground. Mrs. Vance took a step closer, but Kit hid between Bobbie's legs.

"Come here, Roxy," Mrs. Vance cooed, crouching down and reaching out to coax Kit to come to her.

Kit took one tentative step forward, her nose sniffing the air.

"That's it, Roxy," Mrs. Vance said in that sickly voice adults used to talk to babies. "You poor, poor thing. You've been through so much." She shot me a glare before returning her attention back to Kit.

"Come on, my precious little fur baby. Let's go home, shall we?" Still crouched on the floor, which couldn't be easy at her age, she leaned forward, reaching to pat Kit on the head.

A low rumble formed in Kit's throat as she lowered her head. She stood still as a statue until the woman's hand came within striking distance.

It all happened so quickly. Mrs. Vance reached out to grab Kit, while the "precious little fur baby" snarled and snapped as viciously as a hungry mountain lion.

Mrs. Vance screeched, jumping to her feet. "She attacked me!"

"Here, Kit." I patted my chest and reached out. She hopped three feet in the air into the safety of my arms. "It's okay." I snuggled my cheek against her neck and held her close, feeling her little heart pounding in her chest.

Deputy Wallenthorp appeared, hurrying toward us. "What is going on here?"

Kit tucked her head in the opening of my jacket and tried to climb inside.

"They have ruined my late husband's dog." Mrs. Vance held out her hand. "Look, I'm bleeding. I'd like to file charges."

"Against Kit?" I asked.

"Against the two of you," Mrs. Vance huffed.

Wallenthorp cleared his throat. "I thought the dog was yours. Did you want to file charges against yourself?"

If I wasn't mistaken, one corner of his mouth turned up ever so slightly at the question.

"No, of course not. Don't be ridiculous."

"Very well," he said. "Why don't we go into my office and discuss the matter further?"

"I don't want to discuss the matter further. I want my dog. Now."

Deputy Wallenthorp impressed me with his calm manner. "That dog," he pointed at Kit, or rather Kit's fluffy tail, since the rest of her had burrowed into my jacket, "will stay here until ownership is determined. Mrs. Leland has engaged a lawyer to represent her interests, and while it's not required, you may wish to do the same."

"I don't have time for all that." Mrs. Vance narrowed her eyes at me. "You haven't heard the last of me." She turned and stomped out of the room.

I gave her a little wave. "Okey dokey, see ya!" Pulling my jacket open, I whispered, "You can come out now. The mean lady has left."

Kit stayed put, and I couldn't say I blamed her.

Something was odd about that Mrs. Vance. "Deputy Wallenthorp, did she even ask about her husband?"

His eyes widened. "She didn't."

"Too bad you didn't ask for her identification. I mean, how do you even know she's the dead guy's wife?"

"I, um, well." Wallenthorp hurried out the door, I assumed to chase down Mrs. Vance or whatever her name was.

Kit had managed to turn around inside my jacket and poked her head out.

"I don't blame you for biting her," I said, giving her a scratch behind one ear. "I didn't like her either."

Moments later, Wallenthorp returned out of breath. "Her car was parked out front and she drove off before I could get to her. Got a partial plate. Not sure if it'll be enough."

"A car?" Bobbie asked. "Not an SUV? Did it have chains?"

"I don't think so." Wallenthorp eyed me curiously. "Why do you ask?"

"They wouldn't have let her up the hill this morning without chains after the snowfall we had last night."

I nodded. "I'd say that makes her suspect number one, wouldn't you say, deputy?"

Wallenthorp's shoulders slumped. "Follow me."

I tucked Kit under my arm as he led us to a small office in the back of the room. After motioning for us to take a seat, he settled in behind his desk. He opened a folder and shuffled some papers before he picked up the desk phone and dialed.

Identifying himself to the person on the other end of the line, he asked, "When did you notify Jonathan Vance's next of kin?" His scowl deepened as he listened for what seemed like a long time. He said, "I see," several times, then hung up.

Clasping his hands on top of his desk, he said, "Mrs. Vance died three days ago."

"Oh, so that *wasn't* Mrs. Vance who came here today." I didn't feel the need to say, "I told you so."

"That is tragic for their family," Bobbie said solemnly, always the tactful one. "On the bright side, I suppose that means we can take Kit home, unless there are other relatives planning to come out of the woodwork to claim her." She stood to go, so I did the same.

"There's another development, as it turns out, and you might want to be seated when I tell you."

Bobbie sat back down, but I didn't, figuring I could handle whatever he might have to say.

Wallenthorp cleared his throat. "I was just informed by the Riverside P.D. that Jonathan Vance is not dead."

"Huh?" Questions swirled in my mind, the main one being, "Then who was the dead guy I found at the inn?"

"That's something I'd like to know."

Chapter Six

"Jonathan Vance is alive? Are they sure?" I asked. "Did someone talk to him and make sure they had the right guy?" *This time,* I added silently.

Deputy Wallenthorp ran his hand through his thinning hair, clearly exasperated. "As is protocol, we contacted the local authorities to inform Mrs. Vance of her husband's death in person. When they arrived and asked to speak to her, Mr. Vance was getting in the car to attend her funeral."

Bobbie's hand pressed against her chest. "Oh, no."

"Oh, yes. He didn't give me details, but it didn't go well, as you might imagine. The officer wasn't too happy with me, I can tell you."

"How did she die?" I asked. Wallenthorp frowned, but I needed to know. "Hey, the man impersonating her husband was murdered, so I think it's a relevant question."

He hesitated. "Natural causes."

"Are you sure?" I asked. "A lot of things can look like natural causes, but when you take a closer look—"

"You have a lot on your plate," Bobbie cut in. "Why don't we get out of your hair and take Kit home? I promise we'll bring her back if necessary." She held one hand behind her back, and I knew she had her fingers crossed.

Wallenthorp stared at her with tired eyes while he decided. "Fine."

We left before he could change his mind. Once we were outside, we slogged through the snow on our way home.

I tucked Kit inside my jacket to keep her warm. "Why did this guy come to Arrow Springs claiming to be Jonathan Vance? Just to get Kit? I mean, I think she's a great dog, but how much could she possibly be worth to a stranger?"

"Maybe he wasn't a stranger," Bobbie suggested.

"Huh?"

"You said Kit snarled and snapped at him, right? She nipped at Mrs. Vance, too, but only when she tried to grab her."

"You're right. Kit doesn't seem to care for men in general, but she growled as soon as she heard his voice. I got the feeling she *really* didn't like him."

"And, if the real Vance used to own Kit, then I think it's safe to assume that the fake Vance knew the real Vance." Bobbie sounded proud of her deductive skills.

"I suppose that makes sense. But why did the fake Vance want Kit? I'm starting to think there's something unusual about her." I repeated the words I heard through the door of room 281 earlier. "That mutt's worth a lot."

"Excuse me?" Bobbie asked.

"Nothing," I muttered. "Just thinking out loud."

"I'd like to know who the woman was claiming to be Mrs. Vance. I'll call Mr. Fernsby as soon as we get home. Maybe he can help us solve the murder."

"Honestly, I don't care who killed that horrible man. I just want to make sure no one else comes to town trying to take Kit away from us."

Bobbie smiled. "I remember when you first came to Arrow Springs to stay with me. You told anyone who would listen that you didn't want a dog. I guess a lot can change in a few short weeks. Better watch out or people will start accusing you of being softhearted."

"Don't you dare call me soft!" I'd spent my life convincing everyone I knew, including myself, that I was tough as nails. And not the kind that bent when you hit them wrong. "Just because I care about another living creature doesn't make me soft."

"I never said it did." Bobbie laid one hand on my arm. "I'd like to stop somewhere before we head home."

"I hope it's someplace warm." This whole winter weather thing was getting old, and it wasn't even officially winter.

Chapter Seven

Bobbie guided me onto a side street a few blocks past the inn and stopped in front of a storefront.

A bright yellow sign over the door said, "Security Plus," while huge letters painted on the windows announced, "Divorce Surveillance Specialists," "Hidden Cameras," and "Ghost Hunting Gear Sold Here."

"Classy place," I quipped.

"You have no idea." Bobbie headed straight for the front door while Kit sniffed intently at a clump of grass growing out of a crack in the sidewalk. I gave her leash a tug and followed Bobbie inside the store.

The place was set up with glass counters on three sides. Merchandise of all sorts hung on the wall or sat on shelves—cameras, receivers of some sort, and other equipment I couldn't identify.

I nearly jumped when I noticed the man standing motionless by the front window. He held a pair of binoculars to his eyes and seemed to be oblivious to our presence. He had a Clark Kent look to him, in his horn-rimmed glasses, short-sleeved shirt and tie, though he'd have some bulking up to do to fit into Superman's costume.

"Excuse me." I spoke tentatively since he seemed deep in concentration.

"Shh!" He didn't move.

Looking out the window, all I saw was a bookstore. I whispered to Bobbie, "Is that bookstore new?"

She nodded.

"Some bookstore!" The man lowered his binoculars and stepped away from the window. I guessed him to be around my age or maybe early thirties. "I went to third grade with the person claiming to be the owner, but she claims not to remember me. Then I asked her if they had any Ursula K. Le Guin novels, and do you know what she asked me?"

"No," Bobbie said in a hushed tone. "Do tell."

He imitated a woman's falsetto voice. "'Does she write YA?'" He paused and pushed his glasses higher up his nose, obviously outraged by the question. "YA! Not that there's anything wrong with YA, mind you, but who doesn't know that Ursula K. Le Guin is known far and wide for her speculative fiction? Who, I ask you?"

I rose my hand, and he turned toward me as if just noticing my presence.

"Who are you?"

"This is my granddaughter, Kelvin," Bobbie said. "The one I told you about."

"Hey, I'm Whit." I held out my fist for a bump.

"Oh." He stared at my hand, as if he didn't know what to do.

"It's called a fist bump," I explained. "We bump knuckles. Much more sanitary than a handshake and not as intrusive as a hug. I'm not much of a hugger."

"Why?" he asked.

"Why?" I repeated. "Why am I not much of a hugger, or why the fist bump?"

"The latter. It seems an arbitrary and curious custom." He paused as if afraid he'd said the wrong thing. "I'm not objecting, it's just something I've wondered from time to time. I thought you might know."

Kelvin set the binoculars down on one of the glass counters, took off his glasses, and drew a cloth from his breast pocket. As he wiped his glasses, I glimpsed pale, aqua-blue eyes with long, dark eyelashes. It seemed unfair that so many men were running around with gorgeous eyelashes without having to bother with mascara.

He shoved his glasses back on his face as he took a few steps closer to Bobbie. "You didn't tell me she was so..." he murmured, knocking the binoculars off the counter.

As Kelvin bent down to retrieve the binoculars, I asked, "So... what? What did Bobbie not tell you about me?"

Bobbie came to the young man's rescue. "Did we come at a bad time, Kelvin?" She followed him to the back of the shop. "We'd like to ask your advice. It's about our dog." Bobbie gestured to Kit. "She has a microchip—two, actually, as we learned recently. I thought you might know how to disable the tracking capabilities."

After inspecting the binoculars for damage, he put

them in their case, then focused his attention on Bobbie. "The microchips installed in dogs use RFID technology." He must have noticed our blank looks, because he added, "Radio-frequency identification. It takes a scanner to read the information on the chip. Without a scanner, the chip won't provide any information—certainly not location."

"I see," Bobbie said. "How far away will the scanner work?"

"Oh, no more than a few inches."

Bobbie nodded, giving the new information some thought. "What if somebody with a lot of resources wanted to plant a tracking device in a dog like Kit here? Could they do it?"

"Not likely." Kelvin gave Bobbie a friendly smile. It seemed he'd forgotten about whatever might be going on in the bookstore across the street. "The smallest GPS chip currently on the market is about ten millimeters square, unlike the RFID tags they use for dogs which are about the size of a grain of rice."

I'd never gotten the hang of the metric system. "Just how big is ten millimeters?"

"Approximately three eighths of an inch. It would require surgery to implant one in an animal. No one would do such a thing."

"Three eighths of an inch isn't *that* big." Would the dead man, whoever he was, have hesitated to surgically implant a device to track her location? I doubted it. "Is there a way to tell if she has one under her skin?"

Kelvin looked from me to Bobbie, who nodded.

"Would you mind terribly humoring us?" Bobbie asked.

He grinned. "You bet." He stepped behind the counter and returned with a device about the size and shape of a TV remote. He knelt next to Kit, and she immediately growled softly.

"It's okay, girl." I pet her while Kelvin scanned her, waving the wand over and under her from her nose to her tail.

"She's clear," he announced. "Either she doesn't have a tracker or the battery's gone dead. Even the longest lasting batteries only last a few years—most not even that long."

"That's a relief, isn't it, Whit?" Bobbie eyed the device in Kelvin's hand. "How much is one of those, by the way?"

"For you, I'll give you my very best price."

Chapter Eight

Bobbie carried a shopping bag full of equipment she'd bought from Kelvin. The plow had come while we were gone, and the streets were clear, with huge mounds of dirty snow on each side. As we reached the top of the hill, something felt off. A prickle went up my spine as I got out and approached the voluptuous, flaxen-haired woman standing by the front door.

"Whit!" She grinned when she saw me, displaying dazzling white teeth. She wore a short sweater dress, thigh-high boots, and a fur-trimmed coat. Sizing her up—all curves where I was angles and straight edges—I felt a rush of conflicting emotions.

"Tess?"

"Of course, silly." In two long strides, she reached me and enveloped me in a tight squeeze, pillowing me against her ample chest. Thankfully, the hug was brief.

"What are you doing in town?" I wanted to add "at my front door," but I bit my tongue. I'd only met her a few times at the studio, so how did she find out where I was staying?

"I'm scouting locations for a new show. I'd never heard of Arrow Springs, but when someone told me you were holed up here, I thought I'd check it out. This town is charming with a capital C. And just look at the scenery!" With a wave of her arm, she took in the evergreen trees flocked with snow and the white-capped mountains beyond.

"A new show?"

"Set in a small, fictional, mountain town. It's supposed to be in the Pacific Northwest, but the director wants to stay close to home. And now that I've had a chance to look around, I think Arrow Springs is the perfect place for the exterior shots. The downtown area feels frozen in time, with those wood sidewalks. And the general store! Walking around the shops, I felt like I was in a Hallmark movie. I feel like I'm at risk of having a lumberjack sweep me off my feet and convince me to leave my big-city life behind."

"It's really not lumberjack season, but I know a guy who carves animals out of dead trees with a chainsaw. Maybe I could introduce you."

She laughed, a musical sound that bore no resemblance to my snorts and guffaws. "Anyhow... we'll film most of the show on sound stages, but," she paused. "Look at me telling you how filming works."

Kit, having watered a few bushes, now guided Bobbie toward us, tugging hard on her leash. After sniffing Tess's feet, she began rubbing herself against her expensive suede boots, flopping on her back.

"Kit!" I scolded. "Stop doing that."

"I don't mind." Tess bent down to rub Kit's belly. "What a cutie you are."

Bobbie handed me Kit's leash. "Why don't you invite your friend inside out of the cold, and I'll make us something warm to drink." She unlocked the door and went inside.

"Come on in." I waved Tess inside. "That's my grandmother, by the way."

Bobbie stopped by the hall closet. "That's how you introduce me? Sometimes I think you were raised by wolves."

"I always suspected Angela might not be human," I joked.

Bobbie ignored me, pulling off her gloves and reaching a hand to Tess. "I'm Roberta Leland, but please call me Bobbie. All my friends do."

Tess took Bobbie's hand in both of hers in a gesture I'd seen her do many times. She once told me sincerity was the best way to connect with people and once you can fake that, the rest was easy. She insisted she was kidding, but I had my doubts.

"What a lovely home you have, Bobbie." Her voice exuded warmth.

"Why thank you, Tess. Give Whit your coat and come into the kitchen. How does tea sound? Or I can make us some hot cocoa."

"Do you have some herbal tea? I'm weaning myself off caffeine. The body is a temple, and I decided it was time to treat mine better."

I snorted, and Tess gave me a questioning look. "Oh,

you were serious?" Tess had a reputation as a party girl, but maybe she'd changed her ways.

After letting Kit off her leash, I hung our coats in the closet while Tess followed Bobbie into the kitchen. I plopped myself at the kitchen table across from Tess, and Bobbie put the kettle on the stove.

"Maybe you'll be a positive influence on Whit," Bobbie said. "She lives on cinnamon rolls, coffee, and wine."

"Do not," I grumbled.

Tess's smile wouldn't have looked out of place on a saint. "It's okay, Whit. It's almost the new year. A great time to develop new habits. Meditation has helped me achieve a state of inner calm and peace. You should try it."

"I meditate," Bobbie said as she searched through her extensive tea collection. "And do yoga."

"See? Bobbie knows what I'm talking about." A mischievous look replaced her saintly smile. "What do you do for fun in this sleepy town?"

"There's not much to do besides eating and drinking," I admitted. "The hiking and rock climbing are great when it's warmer."

"Doesn't anything exciting happen, at least occasionally?"

"Oh!" I remembered something pretty exciting. "I found a dead body last night."

Tess burst into laughter. When she composed herself, she said, "Oh, that's rich. You always say the most outlandish things, Whit."

"You're right about that." Bobbie found the herbal teabags I'd shoved to the back of the cabinet. "But she's telling the truth this time. A man was murdered, and Whitley and I are going to find out who the killer is before he or she strikes again."

"We are?" I asked.

Tess raised one eyebrow. "You're saying someone was actually murdered? Here in town?"

I nodded. "At the Arrow Springs Inn."

She placed a perfectly manicured hand on her chest. "Aren't you traumatized? I'm sure I would be. Just the thought of seeing someone..." Her voice trailed off, and she shivered.

While I considered telling her about the other two dead bodies I'd come across last month, the teakettle picked that moment to whistle. If Tess had considered moving to Arrow Springs, three murders might change her mind.

Bobbie placed our steaming mugs of tea on the table and joined us. I sniffed mine, disappointed. Chamomile tea was fine at the end of a long day, but I hadn't come close to my required caffeine intake for the day.

Tess wrapped her hands around the warm mug and breathed in the steam. "That's lovely." She took a dainty sip and set the mug down. "Sounds like I missed out on a lot of excitement by not staying at the inn. I'm at the Arrow Lake Cottages, but I'm going home tomorrow."

"Why don't you move from the cottages to the inn?" Bobbie suggested. "It would give Whit and me an excuse to be there during our investigation."

Tess frowned, at least as much as her last Botox injection allowed. "You want me to move into an inn where they just had a murder?"

"They might give you a good rate." I wondered how many guests had checked out as soon as they heard about the dead guy in room 281.

Bobbie gave me a playful smack on the arm. "The man who died was a criminal who had come to Arrow Springs for nefarious purposes. Someone followed him here, they quarreled, and now he's dead."

How much of what Bobbie said had any basis in fact? I'd wait until later to ask her. And who used words like "nefarious"?

"So, you see," Bobbie continued, "it wasn't a random attack. You'll be quite safe at the inn."

"And Bobbie's right. It would give us a good excuse to hang out at the inn and maybe question some of the other guests. I bet someone saw something, even if they don't know it."

Tess gave Bobbie a long, hard stare, then turned her gaze to me. "What, are you two a crime-solving duo now? Like on TV? Do you also refinish furniture or bake cupcakes while solving murders?"

"Bobbie has been known to bake cupcakes, but not nearly often enough, in my opinion."

While Bobbie and Tess chatted, my mind churned with ideas. If Tess stayed at the inn, I might have a chance to find out if the woman I'd seen was really Julia.

In a cheerful, encouraging tone, I asked, "Why don't you stay over the weekend? You don't want to drive back to L.A. in Friday night traffic. The 91 freeway will be awful." When she didn't seem convinced, I threw in a sense of urgency. "With the fresh snow, everyone will head up for the weekend as soon as they clear the roads.

But you better call the inn right away before they're fully booked. Even with the murder, I bet they'll still fill up."

"Maybe..."

"I'll take you to Gypsy's Tavern tonight. Live music and a hot bartender. And who knows? A lumberjack might wander in."

That got a grin and a chuckle out of Tess. "Okay, okay. You've convinced me."

Tess called the inn and arranged to stay for the weekend, then called to cancel her last night at the cottage.

She checked the time on her phone. "I need to get my things from the cottage and go check into the inn. Want to meet me there later? I'm looking forward to checking out the local wildlife." She gave me a wink to let me know she wasn't talking about lions, tigers, or bears.

Now that was the Tess I remembered. "Sounds good. Around seven? We can grab something to eat."

Bobbie showed Tess to the front door and retrieved her coat.

When she handed me mine, I raised my eyebrows. "I don't need my coat. I'm staying in until dinner time."

"I'd like you to drive me to the office to meet with Mr. Fernsby." For Tess's benefit, she explained, "He's the P.I. I'm apprenticing under."

"Is that so?" Tess gave me an approving nod. "You might just have the coolest grandma ever."

<hr />

Twenty minutes later, with Bobbie and Kit in the passenger seat, I pulled into the parking lot of a dingy strip mall. I found a spot in front of the pawn shop, whose peeling sign advertised:

$ FOR IMMEDIATE $ ANY GOLD (BROKEN, OLD OR NEW)

Kit pranced with excitement, tugging at her leash and pulling Bobbie in every direction. Bobbie handed me the leash and headed for the stairs, but I lingered in front of the taco joint. I could almost taste their crispy chicken tacos with extra guacamole.

"Come on," Bobbie called to me from halfway up the stairs. "We'll get tacos later."

Kit and I followed her up the metal steps to the second floor and down a dreary hallway. A sign on one door said Arrow Investigations. Bobbie didn't bother knocking.

We stepped into the small reception room, which held a single desk, chair, and a row of metal filing cabinets. I had enjoyed my time spinning in that chair while Bobbie nagged me to help with the filing. Kit sniffed the floor eagerly, and the moment I let off her leash, she hurried off to inspect every corner of the room.

A door with a frosted glass panel read Bernard Fernsby, Private Investigator. Bobbie pulled one of Kit's favorite chew sticks out of her purse and tossed it across the room, then knocked.

A gruff voice came through the door. "Come in."

Bernard sat behind his oak desk, the central casting version of a grizzled, has-been P.I. Short and overweight, he wore a rumpled shirt and striped silk tie he'd probably owned for decades. He might look like a has-been, but he'd surprised me more than once with his quick mind and ability to get information from the police force and other sources.

Bobbie greeted him. "Good to see you, Mr. Fernsby."

"Hey, Bernie," I cheerfully teased.

"I told you never to call me that," Bernard grumbled.

"You never should have told her not to." Bobbie took a seat across from Bernard. "Now she'll never stop."

My stomach grumbled. "I might stop if someone bought me tacos."

Bobbie shook her head in disapproval of my singular focus. "Is food the only thing you think about?"

"There are other things, but none that I want to share with my grandmother."

Bobbie pulled out a couple of twenties and handed them to me. "We'll have the usual and bring me the change this time."

I had an ulterior motive for my taco errand—a side quest. After putting in our order at the taco joint, I went next door to the pawn shop. The door was locked. Disappointed, I was about to leave when I spotted an intercom with a button labeled "Press here for entrance." I pushed the button and waited.

A woman's voice squawked on the tinny speaker. "Do you have an appointment?"

An appointment? Really?

"No, I'm sorry. I didn't know I'd need an appointment. My name is Whitley Leland and I'm staying with my grandmother over the holidays. I just—"

Before I got to my question, the door buzzed. I pulled it open and stepped inside, immediately struck by a musty smell and the faint hint of cleaning solution.

Fluorescent lights flickered overhead, casting a harsh glow. Shelves lined the walls, cluttered with a hodgepodge of items—musical instruments, electronic devices, and other once-valued possessions.

A burly man behind a counter sorting or inspecting some items in a shallow tray stopped what he was doing. His stern expression as he watched me approach, not to mention the neck tattoos, nearly made me turn and leave, but running a pawn shop must require a tough attitude. Who knew what sort of people frequented the place?

Instead of "May I help you?" he simply said, "Yeah?"

I appreciated efficiency, so I launched right into my cover story. "I just had a question. It's kinda dumb." I did my best impression of a ditsy female. "See, a while back, I gave my boyfriend a ring. Anyway, the other night, he's not wearing it. First, he said he took it off when he was working on his car, and he didn't want to scratch it up or anything. But then he says he lost it."

The man gave me a blank look, so I continued.

"I mean, maybe he did lose it? But maybe he sold it." I cast my eyes downward in a moment of silence for my imaginary crappy relationship. "I don't know how much it was worth, but it was like the only thing I had of my dad's."

"What did it look like?"

I began perusing the items in the display case, which didn't appear to be arranged in any logical way. "It was a thick gold ring with three diamonds. I don't know much about diamonds, but the biggest one was about this big." I held out my pinky and thumb about a quarter inch apart.

"Sounds like somewhere between one and two carats."

"That's worth a lot, right?"

"Could be. Depends on the quality of the diamond." He went into a brief explanation of the three C's: cut, clarity, and color, while I pretended to hang on his every word.

"That's very interesting." I gazed at him as if he were the smartest man I'd ever met, but it didn't seem to have much of an effect. I'd found where the men's rings had been grouped, mostly wedding bands and class rings. "I don't see it here."

"How long ago do you think he would have brought it in?"

I shrugged. "He says he lost it a couple days ago."

He cocked his head and a hint of a smug smile formed on his lips. "If he pawned it, it'd be in the back. He's got thirty days plus a ten-day grace period. But if he sold it to us outright, we hold it for seven days before putting it on sale. We gotta make sure it don't come up stolen."

By now, I'd wandered to the other end of the display case, where women's jewelry lay on a faded velour cloth. How many of these pieces had ended up here because their owners fell on hard times? And how many belonged to relatives who'd passed away? What would they think of their children and grandchildren selling off their prized possessions?

"There's another pawn shop in Big Springs," the brute continued. "You might check them out."

Returning to the other end of the shop, I eyeballed the items in the tray he'd been inspecting. My heart skipped a beat as I focused in on a bright blue sapphire set in a gold locket. Leaning in for a closer look, there was no mistaking it. I'd seen that locket in pictures, including a photo currently framed and displayed on Bobbie's mantel.

"That—" I pointed, barely able to speak.

The salesclerk, if that's what he was, came closer to see what had caught my eye. "Oh, yeah. That's a beaut. Paid a pretty penny for it."

I steadied myself. This was no time to fall apart. "Was it a woman who sold it to you? Around fifty years old with long, wavy reddish-brown hair? Really beautiful?"

He pursed his lips. "No..." His eyes went to the ceiling as he recalled the memory. Before he answered, his eyes darted toward the back of the room. "I really shouldn't give you any info. We pride ourselves on discretion."

Frustrated that he'd suddenly clammed up, I stared at the locket. "The chain is broken."

"Oh, yeah. We got plenty of chains. When it goes on sale, we'll find one to go with it."

"Can I see the locket?"

He leaned over the case, inspecting the attached tag. "We gotta hold it for seven days, like I said."

An older woman, possibly the one whose voice I heard earlier, emerged from a back room. Pushing a lock of steel-gray hair over her ear, she locked eyes with me. Did she sense the desperation I felt?

Her expression told me she'd felt heartache and recognized it in me. "Let her see it, Joe."

"You got it, boss."

She slipped back out of the room. With surprising gentleness, Joe picked up the locket and placed it in my waiting hand.

I stared at it, not able to take my eyes off the delicate

scrollwork surrounding the sapphire. Taking a deep breath to steel myself and willing my hand not to shake, I pressed the clasp and opened it, revealing two aged and faded photographs.

On the left, a handsome, dark-haired man peered at me with eyes I'd seen countless times looking back at me in the mirror.

On the right was a baby picture. A tiny girl in a ruffled dress. I'd seen a copy of that picture in a photo album.

The baby was me.

Chapter Nine

A tear landed on the glass counter. I hadn't realized I was crying. Joe snatched a few tissues from somewhere and handed them to me. I wiped my wet face and blew my nose.

"Thanks."

He stepped back, allowing me some measure of privacy.

"They sold this? It wasn't pawned?" I held up the locket as if there might be some doubt about what item I was talking about.

"Yeah. Sold outright."

"You don't understand." I held the open locket facing him, showing him the pictures inside. I pointed to the baby picture. "That's me."

He gave me an understanding nod but showed no sign of giving me the information I needed.

"And that," I pointed to the other picture. Was I really

ready to say it out loud? It was the first photo I'd ever seen of a man I'd never met. "That man is my father."

My chest constricted and I willed myself not to cry again. I struggled to breathe—in, out, in, out. Couldn't Joe see the agony I was in?

If he did, he didn't show it. "We got privacy laws in this state, not to mention what would happen to our reputation if it got out that we gave out anybody's information."

"Your reputation?"

"Yeah." He glared at me. "Our business depends on our reputation, just like anyone."

"I know who owns this locket, and according to you, that's not the person who brought it to you. This was stolen."

"Then the person who owns it needs to file a police report." He held out his hand for the locket.

"Can I take a picture?"

After a slight hesitation, he said, "Yeah, I suppose so."

I took a few shots with my phone, both of the outside of the locket and, more importantly, the picture of the man inside.

"Assuming no one has reported this stolen, could I buy it?"

He handed me a pad of paper. "Write down your name and number and I'll call you."

"Promise?"

He gave me a "what do you think?" look, but he could tell I wanted to hear his answer out loud. "Yeah. I promise. Hope you got the dough for it." He took back the pad of paper and wrote a number. "That's what it'll go for."

It was a big number, maybe bigger than it would have been if he hadn't seen how desperate I was to have it.

"I got the dough." Truth was, I didn't. But I would get it.

⬦ ⤞

Tacos in hand, I returned to Bernard's office, hoping Bobbie hadn't noticed how long I'd been gone or how shaken I was. If she had, she didn't mention it.

We sat around Bernard's desk eating tacos while they brought me up to speed.

"Mr. Fernsby was able to learn the identity of the man whose body you found," Bobbie said as she unwrapped her taco.

Bernard stared greedily at his tacos, but waited before digging in. "The information has not yet been released to the public, so don't share it with anyone."

I gave him a thumbs up and started eating while he continued.

"His name is Guy Pavlakovich."

I swallowed before asking, "Is that a Russian name?"

"Could be." Bernard kept reading from his notes. "Could be a lot of things. He has a rather checkered past, though he's managed to avoid spending more than a night or two in jail."

"Mr. Fernsby thinks Pavlakovich has connections—maybe organized crime."

"I said he *might* have connections," Bernard corrected my grandmother. "My guess—and it's only a guess—but he might do work for some people with deep pockets."

I crumpled my first taco wrapper and opened the second. "Like the Russian mafia?"

"Perhaps, although the Russian mafia isn't a single organization. More of a loose consortium of gangs or mobs."

"If I were going to do shady stuff for someone who'd pay me lots of money, I'd go to work for a politician. Or a big corporation. I bet they'd pay a lot for someone to do their dirty work."

Bobbie swatted me on the knee. "There you go getting ahead of yourself. What we need is facts."

"She might be onto something." Bernard tapped his pen against his notepad. "That would explain how he managed to stay out of prison."

I liked people who listened to my wild theories. "What we need is to figure out why this guy, what'd you say his name was?"

The corners of Bernard's mouth twitched. "His name was Guy."

"Ha. A guy named Guy. That won't be hard to remember. Now where was I?" I found myself struggling to keep focus after discovering Julia's locket in the pawn shop. "Oh, right. We need to know why Guy wanted Kit so bad."

"That is an excellent point," Bernard scribbled something on his notepad. "Any ideas?"

"Not yet. But when we figure it out, I bet it will tell us why Guy got himself murdered. It might even lead us straight to the murderer."

Bobbie and Bernard thought that over for a moment, probably marveling over my brilliant theory.

Bobbie spoke first. "As long as it doesn't lead the murderer straight to us."

⬦ ⬦

Bernard dug into his first taco, but I wasn't done asking questions. I scooted my chair closer to the desk. "How are this guy Guy and Jonathan Vance connected?"

Bernard cocked his head to one side like a Saint Bernard trying to translate human words into dog language. "They're not, as far as I know. Why would they be?"

"Because Kit started to growl the moment she heard him speak. She knew him. And I can tell you she did not like him at all."

"Hmph." Bernard scratched the back of his head, then reached for a folder, flipping through a few pages. "You're sure it was Pavlakovich she was growling at? Maybe she doesn't like men."

"I'm pretty sure she's okay with most men." I could tell Bernard wasn't convinced, so I went into the other room and grabbed Kit's chew stick. She wagged her tail, thinking we were playing a game.

I waved the stick at her. "Come get it, girl."

Kit followed me back into the inner office where I tossed her stick onto the floor at Bernard's feet. She froze, waiting for him to make the first move.

"Hello, doggy." Bernard reached out a hand and she tentatively approached. "She seems a little afraid of me."

"Yeah, but I think you've passed the test."

One thing Kit loved more than her chew sticks was a

85

new pair of shoes to sniff. After she'd investigated the scent of his leather wingtips, she flopped on her back and rubbed against them.

Bernard leaned down and gave her belly a rub before returning to his notes. "There's nothing in Pavlakovich's background check that indicates how he and Vance would have been connected."

"What about Vance's background check?" I asked.

He shook his head. "I didn't see any reason to do one on him, but I can rectify that pretty quickly."

Bernard swiveled in his chair and slid over to an ancient looking computer. At least, it looked ancient to me, but it seemed to work just fine. Although, when his expression changed, I started to wonder.

"Do you need a floppy disk to run that thing?" I'd heard someone make a similar joke, though I'd never seen a floppy disk in real life. "Are floppy disks actually floppy?"

"Let him work," Bobbie scolded.

His expression changed as he tapped away at the keyboard. "That's interesting," he mumbled.

Bobbie stood and walked around his desk and stood behind him. "What is it?"

"Yeah, what's up?" I threw in for good measure.

"Jonathan Vance owns a house with a few acres of property just outside of Riverside. That's his business address, so I'm guessing that's where he boards and trains his dogs."

"Okay." I felt like he was holding back on the punch-line. "What's interesting?"

"He's in foreclosure."

"Road trip!" I jumped to my feet and held the door open, but no one followed me.

Bobbie and Bernard stared at me like I'd lost my mind.

I threw up my hands, frustrated that the two of them weren't keeping up. "We need to go talk to Vance." A thought hit me like a brick. "Vance's wife is dead."

"Yes," Bernard said. "Unfortunate timing, since the Riverside P.D. went to see her to tell her that her husband had been murdered."

"Quite a coincidence, don't you think?" I wiggled my eyebrows for emphasis.

"Oh..." Bobbie's face lit up, which I hoped meant she got my point. "You're thinking she might not have died from natural causes, aren't you?"

I tapped my nose. "Ding, ding, ding, we have a winner."

Bernard held up a hand. "Now, ladies. Let's not get carried away here. People die all the time. It's not that much of coincidence."

I put my hands on my hips, my legs slightly apart in a power pose. I'd been told it communicated confidence. "I say we go to Riverside and see what we can find out from Vance."

Bobbie didn't seem impressed by my stance. "Who do you think you are? Wonder Woman?"

I sighed and plopped back in the chair. "If we don't do something, Vance is going to come for her." I pointed at Kit, who apparently had lost interest in her chew stick. She stood on her back legs the way she did when she wanted a treat. I pointed at the ground and said, "Down."

She dropped to the floor and slid on her belly toward me. I tried another command. "Up."

Bernard watched her roll over. "She obviously knows a few tricks, even if you haven't mastered the commands. Is that why Vance wants her back so badly?"

"I bet she was the star of the show." I patted my lap and Kit jumped up. At least that was one command she understood. "What'd you say his business was called? Stunt Dogs... Spectacular?"

"Extravaganza." Bernard seemed to ponder something. He placed his hands flat on his desk, one on his notepad and one on the folder holding all the details about Guy's murder. "I think you're right, Whitley."

"I love how that sounds." I grinned, savoring the moment. "Um... what exactly am I right about?"

"We need to question Vance, and it would be best done in person. But let's not rush into anything. We need to get our ducks in a row first. We may only get one chance at him."

"Great." I stood up again. "Grab the ducks and we'll strategize in the car."

"Whitley." Bernard's tone turned fatherly. "They haven't fully cleared the roads yet, and there's another storm on the way. Even if we're able to drive down the mountain this afternoon, we might not get back up tonight."

"I'm willing to risk it."

Unfortunately, the two fuddy-duddies weren't.

Chapter Ten

I dropped off Bobbie at home and headed out to do some shopping. My leggings, jeans, and boots were fine for daily life around town, but I wanted something nice to wear when I got together with Tess that evening.

Most of the stores offered items to appeal to tourists, mostly souvenirs and gift items, but the unimaginatively named Arrow Springs Footwear and Boots had a great selection of quality shoes. I'd made some good tips on my last bartending shift, and figured I deserved to treat myself.

I fell in love with a pair of fur-trimmed, ankle-high booties, but after looking at the price tag, I settled for a fur-free pair. Next, I stopped in at Arrow Silver Smiths and picked out a new pair of earrings.

Stepping outside into the bright winter sun, I wasn't ready to head home yet, so I turned toward Sugarbuns as if drawn there by an invisible force.

"No," I told myself. "No more cinnamon rolls for you." An older woman gave me a funny look, so I gave her a smile, and said, "They're really good cinnamon rolls." She pursed her lips and hurried past.

Turning down the next street to avoid my favorite bakery, I found myself in front of Security Plus. My curiosity and a desire for a distraction that didn't involve warm, gooey pastries sent me through the front door.

No one greeted me, which gave me a few moments to look around. I peered into the glass cases, wondering what all the various electronic gadgets did. Making my way toward the back of the shop, I spotted what looked like a small drone. When I picked it up, Kelvin appeared out of nowhere.

He hurried over, grabbed it from me, and put it behind the counter. "Sorry. You can never be too careful."

"What was that thing?"

"It's a partially autonomous unmanned aerial vehicle powered by a lithium polymer battery," he said. "It's equipped with a high-resolution camera with image stabilization."

"Right." That was way more than I needed to know. How should I approach my next question? "What's Bobbie up to? Who is she surveilling?" I wasn't even sure that was a word, but he didn't raise an eyebrow.

"That," he said. "is privileged information."

"What, like attorney-client privilege? But you're not an attorney. And you're definitely not a priest." I paused, imagining him in a clerical collar. "You're not, are you?"

He shook his head. "All the equipment you see here in

the shop is perfectly legal when installed according to local, state, and federal rules and regulations."

"I see. Are you saying if Bobbie is using them in some sort of sketchy way, you wouldn't have any personal knowledge about that."

He seemed to consider my statement, and it took him several moments to answer. "No comment."

"Dude." I leaned back against the counter. "That's the most incriminating thing you can say. What you want to say is, 'I don't know what you're getting at,' preferably in an accusing way. Get the other person on the defensive. Go ahead and try it."

His brow wrinkled in confusion. "Try what?"

"Say, 'I don't know what you're getting at,' but make it sound like you're really offended."

"I don't know what you're getting at," he repeated in a monotone.

"Not bad, really. A very sincere delivery. It just might work." I was starting to have fun. "Now, once more, only try saying it more forcefully."

We went back and forth several times with a few different phrases until I thought he'd mastered plausible deniability.

"Great job." I still wanted to find out what Bobbie was up to, so I asked him directly.

His eyebrows rose. "How would I know what she has planned?"

I sighed. "Well done." I'd taught him too well. "Okay, can you at least show me what she bought? Or is that against the spy code of ethics or something?"

After a moment of indecision, he began pointing out

the items Bobbie had purchased recently. There'd been quite a few—mostly surveillance equipment: cameras, GPS tracking devices, and remote voice recorders.

"Can you show me what sort of surveillance cameras she bought?"

He went behind the counter and retrieved what looked like a phone charger plug. "This is one of my best sellers." He pointed to a small dot next to where you'd plug in a USB cable. "See that?" He held it closer to me until it was inches from my nose. "That's a camera."

"No!" I never would have guessed. "How far away can you be and still see what's going on?"

"You could see most of what's happening in an average sized living room. It's not the sharpest image, but for the price it's a great value."

"What about for outdoors?" I didn't know how far Bobbie had gone in her surveillance mission, but knowing how many cameras she'd bought might give me a clue.

Kelvin reached back and retrieved a robot-like device from a shelf, handing it to me. "This one has a high-resolution image sensor with advanced low-light performance. Notice the rugged housing that protects against harsh weather or tampering."

"Okay, I'll take your word for it." I took a closer look. "It reminds me of Wall-E's girlfriend."

"EVE." He grinned. "That movie is what first got me interested in robotics."

"Is that what your degree's in?" I asked, being polite, but also curious about how Kelvin ended up in a spy shop in a small mountain town.

"Yes, that's what I studied for my bachelor's degree."

He took the little robot camera from me and put it back on the shelf. "My master's is in data analysis."

"Sounds..." I stopped myself from saying "nerdy," and instead said, "interesting."

He narrowed his eyes at me. "You don't really think it's interesting."

"I don't?" I thought for a moment. "No, I suppose I don't, but that's the sort of thing people say to be polite, don't they? I usually say the first thing that enters my mind, but that's gotten me into a lot of trouble over the years. But data analysis *might* be interesting if I knew more about it."

He shook his head, and a smile played at the corner of his mouth. "It's really not. But now I'm getting into A.I. and that's fascinating. We use A.I. for all sorts of things without being aware of it, like our smart phones or cars that stay in the lane without having to steer them."

"A.I.?"

"Artificial intelligence." He gave me a half smile-half grimace. "Sorry, I get carried away sometimes talking about the newest technology."

"No worries. Is that what made you open up this shop? All the cool devices and stuff?"

"Oh, sure," he said, but I got the feeling there was more to the story. "Sometimes life doesn't quite turn out the way you expect."

"No kidding. Well, thanks for your time. You can go finish building your robot or whatever you do back there."

His face lost color. "I'm not building a robot."

I smiled, hoping to set him at ease. "It was a joke. Not

a very good one, I admit, but it's the best I could come up with on short notice."

"Wait a sec." Kelvin reached into one of the glass cabinets and retrieved a pen, handing it to me. "On the house."

"Um, thanks?" I flipped it over in my hand, expecting to see "Spies R Us" or something similar printed on the side. "You can never have too many pens."

He leaned on the counter and spoke softly, like he was telling me a secret. "It's not an ordinary pen."

"It's not?"

"Press here..." He clicked a tiny, recessed button on the side. "That will send a message to anyone you've programmed to receive it. It will even send your GPS signal to them."

"Wow, cool. Like a mobile bat signal." I took a closer look at the relatively normal looking pen. "Is there a keyboard that pops up somewhere so you can program it?"

Kelvin chuckled, probably figuring I'd made a joke. "You set it up on your phone."

"Uh, huh." I knew enough about technology to get by, but that was about it.

"Want me to do it for you?" he asked.

I entered my passcode on my phone and handed it to him. He did his magic and within a minute or so handed it back to me.

"Who's it going to message if I find myself in deep doo-doo?" I asked.

He grinned. "Me."

I shook my head slowly. "You may live to regret that, Kelvin."

Back in my bedroom, I picked out an outfit for my evening out with Tess. I made extra effort on my appearance, hoping not to fade into the background as I usually did in her company. Would a black leatherette mini skirt do the trick?

Unfortunately, the mini skirt no longer fit over my hips, so I switched to leggings and a low-cut top. I fussed with my grown-out pixie cut, too short to curl and too long to spike. Why was I trying so hard to compete with Tess? I'd be just as gorgeous as her if I had her money, her ample curves, her perfect hair... People always told me I was so lucky to be "skinny" but one look at her and I wished my body wasn't so straight up and down.

I shuffled down the hall in my stocking feet to the kitchen where Bobbie stirred a pot on the stove.

"Smells good." I considered canceling my plans with Tess and staying home, but I had other reasons to visit the Arrow Springs Inn. If I could find Julia, I could corner her and make her talk to me and answer my questions. I had a lot of questions.

Bobbie ladled something from the pot into a bowl and carried it to the table. "You look nice."

"You always say that." It was one of my favorite things about her. "Can I borrow some mascara? I think mine dried up in 2012."

She chuckled and gave me specific directions where to find the samples she collected. "You can take anything from the purple zippered bag, but nothing else." As if she wasn't sure I'd heard her, she repeated, "Nothing else, understand?"

"Got it."

Freshly made up, I ignored Bobbie's warnings about the storm headed our way and drove into town, arriving at the inn an hour early. I wanted to hang out in the lobby and people watch before getting together with Tess.

I stepped into the warm, welcoming lobby of the Arrow Springs Inn and headed straight for the crackling fireplace. A couple snuggled on a loveseat facing the fire. They might have wanted privacy, but if so, they could always get a room.

I pulled an oversized armchair closer to the fire to get warm.

A male voice behind me said, "I suppose that chair's not big enough for both of us."

I turned to see Henry pulling off his parka, his cheeks rosy from the cold. "You could always sit on my lap."

His cheeks flushed even redder, and he seemed at a loss for words for a moment. "I guess I'll get my own chair. That is, if you don't mind me joining you."

My purpose for coming early was to keep an eye out for Julia, not to flirt with a guy who would probably leave town in a few days, never to be seen or heard from again. But then, maybe I could do both. "Are you staying here?"

"Yes. Just checked in today."

A plan formed in my mind. "Pull up a chair."

He maneuvered another armchair next to mine. "They're heavier than they look."

"Really? I hadn't noticed," I teased. After asking him a few questions, I learned he lived in northern California and worked for a tech company. "What brought you to Arrow Springs? Surely, you're not here for business."

"No. I needed a break somewhere off the beaten track, and this seemed like a good fit."

"I see. Can I ask you a question?"

"You just did."

"Ha ha." I gave him a half-hearted smirk. "Have you seen a woman around town with long, auburn hair, around my height and build, but about twenty years older? She might be staying here."

"Not that I've noticed."

"You would have noticed. She's really beautiful. Unless... that is..."

He laughed. "Unless what? Unless I don't notice beautiful women? I noticed you, didn't I?"

"I was your bartender at the time, and you wanted a drink. You would get awfully thirsty if you didn't notice bartenders."

"Good point." He leaned back in his chair. "I would have noticed you even if you were sliding down a hill on your butt."

My eyes widened. "Someone caught me on camera. I knew they would. Did it go viral?" I grabbed my phone, hoping to minimize the damage to my reputation and career. "What's it on, TikTok?"

He laughed again. Either he laughed a lot, or I was especially funny tonight. "The other bartender at Gypsy's told me about it. I stopped in last night hoping to run into you again, but he told me you only fill in from time to time."

"Elijah. That snake." He'd be hearing from me later,

and he could forget about me covering for him on Christmas Eve.

"Uh oh. Looks like I got him in trouble. If you chew him out, would you mind not mentioning my name? I'd hate to get 86'd from the place for having a big mouth."

"Well... I suppose I could say someone else told me. As long as we're doling out favors, I wonder if you might do me one."

His smile was kinda sexy, and I wondered why I hadn't noticed it before. "What would that be? Maybe keeping an eye out for a certain beautiful redhead?"

"Auburn. More brown than red."

"And you think she's staying here at the inn?"

I gave his question some thought. "I'm starting to doubt it. It's not a very good place to hide out, now that I think about it."

"And this woman is hiding? From who?" He raised his eyebrows. "You?"

I forced a laugh and slapped his leg in what I hoped seemed like a playful gesture. "Of course not." Thinking quickly, I came up with what I hoped was a plausible cover story. "She doesn't even know I'm staying in town. Otherwise, she would have gotten in touch. To tell the truth, I'm not all that sure the woman I saw is really her. I might have imagined it."

We were interrupted by the arrival of Tess, looking even more stunning than usual in an azure blue wrap dress. She'd spent some time forcing her blonde hair into waves, made shiny by some expensive grooming products, no doubt.

"Hey Whit." Tess perched on the arm of my chair. "Who's your friend?"

I introduced them. "Henry and I met the other night at Gypsy's Tavern."

"Whit was my bartender," Henry added.

Tess's eyes widened. "Since when do you tend bar? You are one surprise after another." She leaned closer to Henry. "Did you know that Whit and her grandmother are private investigators?"

"We're not," I quickly corrected her. "Bobbie is apprenticing with a local P.I. I'm just in it for the tacos."

Tess laughed and leaned over to give me a one-armed hug. "I just love your non-sequiturs." She focused on Henry again. "You never know what's going to come out of this girl's mouth."

"I'm hungry." I stood, hoping that would be a hint for us to leave.

"What about your friend?" Tess glanced back at Henry, a flirtatious smile on her full, red lips. "Maybe he's hungry, too."

"No," Henry shook his head unconvincingly. "I don't want to butt into your girls' night out."

"I can't speak for Whit, but my goal for the evening was to pick up a couple of hot men to hang out with." Tess fluttered her eyelashes at Henry. "Looks like we're halfway to our goal."

I suppressed a groan. Where did she pick up her dialog? Henry seemed to appreciate it, so I kept my opinion to myself.

"Yes," I said, unenthusiastically. "You should come."

"Well, if you insist..."

Henry got up and brushed the non-existent wrinkles from his merino wool slacks. His v-neck sweater, obviously cashmere, made me want to stroke his arm to see if it was itchy. With Tess along, she'd probably be the one doing the stroking, leaving me as a third wheel.

Pulling on his jacket, he made a suggestion that shook me to my soul. "How about the Gastro Gnome? The guy at the front desk told me I should check it out."

"No!" I hoped I'd heard him wrong.

Tess stopped in the middle of putting her coat on. "What's wrong, Whit?"

"You don't understand," I told them. "It's a gnome-themed restaurant."

Tess grinned. "What a kick!"

"I've sworn to myself never to set foot inside that place ever again. It's nightmare inducing."

Henry gave me a reassuring pat on the back. "We'll be there to make sure none of the gnomes attack you or threaten to settle in your garden. C'mon. It sounds fun."

The two of them ganged up on me until my resolve weakened. Besides, I couldn't let Tess go with Henry alone. I hadn't decided if I was interested in him, but I at least wanted a chance to decide before she swooped in and made him forget he ever met me.

"You two are going to live to regret your decision," I groused. "I already do."

Chapter Eleven

The restaurant, like most businesses in our little town, was a short walk away.

Tess grabbed my arm and leaned in to whisper. "He's a snack. You should go for it." When I didn't respond, she added, "If you don't, I will."

"I like to take things a bit slower than you do," I whispered back.

"Just remember, you snooze you lose."

One of Bobbie's aphorisms should come in handy right now, but all I could think of was, "Haste makes waste."

"Yeah, I wouldn't mind making waste of a weekend with him," she muttered, and I gave her an elbow to her ribs. "Ow."

"What are you two conspiring about?" Henry asked, catching up with us.

"Oh, look." I pointed at the red-hatted statues surrounding their chosen restaurant. "We're here."

Tess squealed delightedly. "You weren't kidding! Look at all the adorable gnomes."

Henry held the door open, and I reluctantly followed Tess inside. The greeter hurried over to us in a tall, pointed red hat and belted tunic. He led us to a curved booth in the back where Tess insisted Henry sit between us.

Our server arrived promptly with menus. "Welcome to Gastro Gnome, where all our dishes are gnome-made and gnome-licious." She recited the specials—the Garden Patch salad with edible flowers and micro greens, a Forest Floor risotto with wild mushrooms—then recommended Gnome-on-a-Stick skewers with chicken or tofu.

I found her last suggestion disturbing. "Do you have beef stew?"

"We always have beef stew," she said with a wide smile. "We're known for it all over town."

"With biscuits?" I asked. If they were out of biscuits, I'd walk home.

"All you can eat," she cheerfully answered.

I grudgingly admitted to the others that the stew was good, so we ordered three bowls, which arrived moments later along with a basket of steaming hot biscuits.

As I slathered butter on my first biscuit, I let Tess lead the conversation.

"So, Henry. Were you at the inn when Whit found the dead guy?"

Henry's spoon hovered halfway to his mouth. "Dead guy?"

"Yeah, didn't you hear about it?"

He shook his head. "I was staying at a friend's cabin

about a mile up the road. Great location, but I wanted to stay in town, so I kept checking every day to see if the inn had any cancellations. They didn't until today. I guess now I know why."

"Yeah, lucky for you and me, right?"

"Tess!" I nearly dropped my biscuit. "How can you say that?"

"Oh, I didn't mean it was lucky that someone died, just lucky that we could get rooms."

"Wait." Henry put his spoon down before he'd even gotten to taste the stew. He glanced at the family at the next table and lowered his voice. "Did you say Whit found the... body?"

"And her grandmother told me she's going to find out who killed him. Isn't that a hoot?" She gave me a pointed look. "Not the body, Whit. Your grandmother." She turned her attention back to Henry. "Tell me more about this friend you were staying with. Is it a good friend?"

He nodded and stuffed a spoonful of stew in his mouth, mumbling, "Mmm, good."

"Arrow Springs is the perfect place for a romantic getaway, don't you think?" Tess didn't wait for him to answer. "What happened? Did you and your *friend* have a fight?"

Henry laughed, catching on to Tess's implication. "He let me use it because it was vacant all week, but I didn't want to take advantage of his generosity. I had only planned to stay a few days, but I kinda fell in love with the place. And these days, I can work from pretty much anywhere." He snatched another biscuit from the basket, and I looked around for the server to bring us more.

"Is that so?" Tess's smile told me she was up to something. "I guess that means you could move up here permanently if you wanted to."

Henry had just shoved half a biscuit in his mouth, so he answered with a noncommittal shrug.

"I'll be moving back to L.A. after the new year," I announced, for both their benefit. "As soon as I go back to work at the studios."

Tess nudged me. "Really?"

I turned to face her. "What do you mean, 'really'? I'm one of the best stunt performers in the business, Tess."

"Oh, sure. I didn't mean anything." She leaned over Henry to pat my hand like I was an upset child. "I didn't blame you for flipping that director on his back, but you know how the business is." In a cheerful voice, she added, "Glad to hear everything's blown over."

I stewed, but I didn't want to get in it with Tess in front of Henry, so I let it drop. Luckily, Henry seemed to have other things on his mind.

Henry lowered his voice to a whisper. "How'd you happen to find a dead body?"

"I went to talk to him, and he was dead."

"Who was he?"

"That's a funny story. I mean, not laugh-out-loud funny, of course, but it turned out he wasn't who he said he was." I didn't trust either of them not to blab, so I wasn't about to tell them the whole story. "He pretended to be someone I had business with. We're still trying to figure out why."

Henry opened his mouth to ask another question, but

Tess spoke first. "Let's bail you guys. Whit promised me a night on the town. Where's the action?"

Henry grabbed the check and insisted on paying. "I've been here for days, and the closest thing I've found to action is Gypsy's Tavern."

"That's where your friend tends bar, right?" Tess grinned at me. "I definitely want to meet him."

We slid out of the booth and pulled our jackets on.

Was I interested in Elijah? Or Henry? I might as well see which one Tess liked best before making up my mind. An awful thought occurred to me—what if she went after both?

How was I supposed to compete with gorgeous?

Henry led the way as Tess took his arm and I straggled behind. The sign over my favorite watering hole still said, "Gypsy's Tavern," so that's what I'd keep calling it until told otherwise.

He held the door open and waited for me. "Having trouble keeping up?"

I wanted to tell him I could kick his butt without breaking a sweat, but I kept quiet. Maybe I'd show him later if he made any more sarcastic comments.

Elijah stood behind the bar and glanced up when we entered.

"Hey, Whit." His gaze went from me to Henry and stopped when he eyed Tess. His mouth dropped open slightly, but he recovered quickly, giving her a wide smile. "I don't think we've met before."

Tess returned his smile and batted her lash extensions. "No, we haven't. I wouldn't have forgotten meeting you."

My mood improved as I quickly realized I'd have

Henry to myself for the evening as Tess and Elijah made goo-goo eyes at each other. Watching them made me want to throw up, but it beat being a third wheel.

Elijah made Tess a specialty cocktail and named it after her. "Whenever I make 'The Tess,' I'll think of you," he said as he set a pink-hued martini in front of her.

I chuckled to myself, since I'd heard him say the same thing to a number of women. She beamed, so I kept that information to myself for now.

Tess took a few selfies with Elijah, then turned her attention to Henry and me. "Let me get a picture of the two of you."

Henry froze. "You won't post it online, I hope. I don't want my boss to think I'm out partying when I told him I'm on a working vacation."

"Like... having a good time is against their code of conduct?" Tess called out to Elijah. "Henry needs a refill."

"That will be my third." Henry held out a hand as if that would stop Tess.

"Glad you can still count." Tess grinned and leaned closer to Henry. "I promise I won't post it anywhere if you don't want me to, but you two make such a cute couple, and I'd like something to remember this night."

"Besides a hangover?" I asked.

Tess laughed and held up her phone. Henry put his arm around my shoulder, and I could smell his cologne or some fancy soap he'd used. My pulse quickened, and I told myself to calm down. For all I knew, he had a girlfriend back home.

"Closer, you two," Tess coaxed. "And Whit, try to look like you're having fun, okay?"

"I am having fun," I said, frowning.

Tess sighed as if dealing with a petulant child. "Henry, did you know Whit is one of the best stunt performers in the business? Maybe *the* best."

She'd probably just said it to get a smile out of me, but it worked, and she got the picture.

"I'll text it to you," she said with a wink.

"How'd you get into stunt work?" Henry asked.

It didn't take much to get me to talk about my favorite subject. I gave him a quick summary of my gymnastics career and Parkour hobby.

As soon as I mentioned Parkour, he got excited. "I've seen videos of those guys jumping from one building to the next and all kinds of crazy stuff. You really did that?"

"Still do from time to time." I'd gotten out of the habit lately, and not just because of the weather. My whole life had been turned upside down, and I'd yet to find my equilibrium. "You should check out my social media." I flipped a napkin over. "I'll write down my @ if someone has a pen. Oh, wait. I have one right here."

I pulled out the pen that Kelvin had given me. "Check this out. See this little button on the side? If I'm in trouble, all I have to do is press it and help will come."

"Like for someone to come rescue you?" Tess asked. "You never struck me as the type who needed rescuing."

"I don't." I frowned. "It wasn't my idea."

Henry's brows drew together. "Like the police?"

"No, though that would be helpful." I stared at the pen. "There's this guy in town who sells security equipment."

"Is he cute?" Tess asked.

"You have a one-track mind, don't you?" I thought a moment. "I suppose so. And as a bonus, he can fix your computer or probably make you a website."

"Let me see," Tess held out her hand.

I held it up just out of her reach. "Here's the one side." I flipped it over. "And here's the other."

"No, I want to hold it." She snatched it from me.

"Hey, give it back. And don't—"

"Oops." Tess's eyes widened in feigned remorse.

"Oops, what?"

"I'm sorry," Tess said, though I could tell she wasn't. "I accidentally pressed the button. Now we'll just have to wait and see if your nerdy boyfriend shows up."

"He's not my boyfriend," I protested. "And that wasn't a very nice thing to do."

It hadn't occurred to me to ask Kelvin what to do if I pressed it accidentally. Maybe the thing didn't work. As the minutes ticked by, I began to think that was the case and forgot all about Kelvin.

Elijah made me another old fashioned, and Henry and I chatted over drinks and bar nuts. Tess had lost Elijah's attention as the place filled up with a late-night crowd, so she honed in on our conversation.

The jazz quartet was setting up when the front door flew open. Kelvin rushed in, looking around frantically. He spotted me through his fogged-up glasses and hurried over to the bar.

"Are you okay?" His voice shook a little, and I felt guilty having dragged him out on a cold, snowy night. He must have rushed, because he seemed underdressed for the weather. Of course, he didn't have Bobbie to remind him to wear a hat, gloves, and scarf.

"Sorry, Kelvin. It was her fault." I pointed at Tess. "I was just showing her the pen, and—"

"I couldn't help myself," Tess interrupted, sliding off her barstool. "I'm Tess, by the way. And you're a friend of Whit's? She's never even mentioned you, and yet here you are, coming to the rescue. How chivalrous."

Henry gave Kelvin a side glance. "How, exactly, were you planning to save the day?"

"I—" Kelvin stammered. "I thought—"

"Don't listen to him," Tess said. "As long as you're here, why don't you join us? Come sit next to me."

Kelvin reminded me of a deer in headlights, and I needed to get him away from my friends before they did any real damage.

I tapped his arm. "Let's go outside for a minute."

"No, that's okay. I'll go." His eyes darted to Henry and Tess, then he turned and headed for the door.

I followed him, and as soon as we were away from the others, I said, "I'm really sorry." I wanted to add that I was sorry my friends were condescending toward him, but that might make things worse.

"Do you need someone to get you home?" he asked. "I hope you're not driving."

"Nah, I'm fine. But thanks for being concerned. And thanks for coming to my rescue."

He gave me a reluctant smile, then reached out his fist. I gave it a bump, then watched him walk out the door and out into the snowy evening.

When I returned to the bar, Tess had moved into my

seat. I took the stool on the other side of Henry. I sipped on my drink while they chatted. After about an hour, the crowd thinned, and Elijah returned his attention to Tess.

I slid off the stool and wobbled a bit. Kelvin was right —I wouldn't be driving home. "I've had a long day, and Bobbie and I have plans for tomorrow, so I think I'm going to head on out."

Henry stood. "I'm going to call it a night, too. I'll walk you out."

Elijah and Tess barely noticed us leaving. Tess had switched from 'The Tess' to tequila shots. So much for "the body is a temple."

Henry stopped at the door and turned back, whispering in my ear. "Should we ask Elijah to make sure she gets back to the inn, okay?"

"Nah, I wouldn't worry. She's not letting him out of her sight until morning."

It must have been snowing the entire time we'd been inside. It came down in thick, fluffy flakes, covering the ground in a blanket of white. I pulled the hood of my parka over my head, shoved my hands into my pockets, and headed down the wooden sidewalk.

When I realized Henry hadn't followed me, I turned back to find out why. He wore a goofy smile as he walked out from the shelter of the sidewalk's overhang. Flakes landed in his hair as he reached out his bare hands to catch one.

I laughed and headed back to retrieve him. "What— have you never seen snow coming down before?"

He turned to me, his eyes wide with awe. "I never have. It's beautiful!"

"And you're going to be soaked if you don't get out of it." I grabbed his warm hand and pulled him back to the covered sidewalk. "Snow turns into water when it melts, in case you aren't aware."

He pulled me to the edge of the sidewalk and wrapped his arm around my waist. We stood in silence, watching the snow drift onto the road.

I felt giddy, lost in the moment, but I knew getting carried away was risky. "We need to get going. I'm going to have to walk home and come back for my car in the morning."

He pulled me closer until I could feel his breath on my face. "You could stay with me."

I laughed, hoping it sounded playful. "Slow down, turbo." A one-night stand wasn't what I was looking for. I wanted more. Was Henry looking for more?

His smile evaporated abruptly. "You're right. But I'm not letting you walk home alone."

As we hurried up the road, slogging through the wet snow, I thought of how warm and cozy the inn would be tonight, especially with warm arms wrapped around me.

Why did I have to choose tonight to be sensible?

Chapter Twelve

When I shuffled into the kitchen the next morning, Bobbie looked like she'd been waiting for me.

"It's about time you got up."

"Stop yelling, please." I held my hands over my ears.

She crossed her arms over her chest. "Do you want to tell me about the man asleep on our sofa?"

A quick peek in the living room, and the events of the previous evening came back to me. I'd insisted that it wouldn't be safe for Henry to walk back to the inn in the heavy snow. Somehow, I'd had the presence of mind to offer him the sofa and not invite him to share my bed.

He lay fast asleep on his back under the afghan with his mouth open and one arm hanging off the side of the sofa. A bump under the afghan moved, and Kit stuck her head out. She seemed to change her mind, and burrowed back next to Henry's warm body, curling up next to one of his legs.

"That's Henry," I explained. "He's staying at the inn. The snow was really coming down last night when we left Gypsy's, so he walked me home."

"He's pretty hunky. I might have stayed with him at the inn if I were you."

I made a face but changed the subject. "Coffee."

"Hair of the dog might be more effective," Bobbie said, "but I have something even better."

"No." I held up a hand as if that could stop her. "Not one of your hangover remedies."

Bobbie ignored me and whipped up an inky-brown concoction that she placed in front of me. "Drink that, and I'll pour you a cup of coffee."

I held my nose. I'd just brought the glass to my lips when Henry appeared in the doorway.

"Good morning." He smiled bashfully at Bobbie. "You must be Whit's grandmother. I've heard a lot about you. I'm Henry."

Bobbie grinned, a twinkle in her eye. "I haven't heard a thing about you. Are you new in town?"

"Sit down." I pulled out a chair for Henry. "You might as well have a cup of coffee while she grills you. I'm going to take a shower."

When I returned to the kitchen, Bobbie and Henry seemed to be getting along like old friends. I poured myself another cup of coffee.

Bobbie checked an app on her phone and announced that the roads were clear. "And no more snow in the forecast, at least for today."

"I need to walk into town to get my car." I nudged Henry. "Ready to go?"

We bundled up and stepped outside. The snowplow hadn't come up our street yet, but as heavy as the snow had been coming down, there were only six inches or so on the ground.

We trudged off into town. "Thanks for last night and letting me stay over."

"Yeah, thanks for walking me home." I pulled my cap down lower, making sure my ears and forehead were completely covered. "I forgot what a bad influence Tess can be. I suppose I thought she might have changed."

"Bobbie's really great. Not sure how many grand-mothers would have reacted that way finding a strange man on her sofa."

"She's the best. You don't even know the half of it." I paused, not sure whether to say more. Maybe I felt chatty after two cups of coffee. "You know how people say they love you, but you wonder if they really mean it? Or you hear the words, but you don't feel them? There are two people I can feel in my gut that they love me. Or rather, one person and one dog."

"Let me guess. Bobbie and Kit?"

Something in my chest tightened. "If anything ever happened to either of them..."

Henry seemed to realize I could benefit from a change of subject. "Tess and Elijah really hit it off. Maybe she'll move up here. I'm sure you'd like having one of your friends in town."

I gave him a side eye. "I've finally learned the differ-ence between friends and acquaintances. There should be another word for people who were in-between—you know, the people you hang out with and do stuff with."

"Things were easier when we were kids, weren't they? You had playmates, pals, buddies, and school friends, and then you had your *real* friends."

I thought about that. "Yeah. Tess is like a playmate—that's the perfect word for her. Not that I can use it in conversation or people might think she posed for a girly magazine."

Henry chuckled. "Let's not start that rumor. She might never forgive us."

We reached the inn and Henry gave me a hug—not too tight, not too long. I felt a little disappointed, but he'd be leaving town soon anyway. I'd forgotten to ask him when he planned to return home.

I found my car underneath a layer of snow and cleared off the windshield enough to drive home. The main road had been plowed, and I made it up the hill to the house easily.

Stepping inside and taking off my wet shoes, I found Bobbie in the kitchen, scribbling on a notepad. She'd made a pile of snacks, and I knew what that meant.

"Road trip!" I needed more coffee first, so I shuffled on over to the coffeepot and filled my mug, doctoring it with extra cream and sugar.

Bobbie checked her to-do list. "Why don't you call Mr. Fernsby and let him know we'll pick him up at the office in half an hour?"

"Bernard's coming with us? I was hoping for a grandmother-granddaughter outing."

"How sweet." Her smile told me I'd scored extra brownie points, which I hoped to redeem for actual brownies. "Mr. Fernsby is the one with the P.I. license, remember? We'll want him there if things get hairy."

"Are you expecting trouble?"

"Just call him, please." She took her coffee and list to the kitchen table while I went into the living room to look for my phone.

"Don't forget to pack the trail mix." I went into the living room to look for my phone. "And the Cheetos."

At the word Cheetos, Kit crawled out from under the afghan that Henry had neatly folded on the sofa. I pulled my phone off the charger and called Bernard, letting him know our ETA.

Returning to the kitchen, I asked, "What about Kit?" I didn't expect we'd be gone all that long, but she couldn't be trusted at home alone. "I don't think we should take her to see Vance. He might not want to let us leave with her."

Bobbie didn't bother looking up from her list. "Jenna is coming over to stay with her and make sure she takes her walks."

"With Mr. Whiskers?" That didn't sound like the best idea to me. "Kit and that cat hate each other."

"Which means that Kit will spend the day hiding under the sofa instead of sneaking out of the house."

"Good point."

A half hour later, Bobbie and I headed out to pick up Bernard at his office. He insisted on sitting in the back, and the two of them strategized while I navigated the winding roads back to civilization. I felt like a hired driver, paid in trail mix and Cheetos. I'd have to ask for a raise.

Nearly two hours later, we turned down a street lined with patchy grass, stubby palm trees, and huge gray boulders. Hard to believe we were in a city of three hundred thousand people and less than an hour from Los Angeles.

"I don't see any addresses," Bobbie muttered, sounding worried. "Or houses, for that matter."

"The GPS will tell us when we're there."

At that moment, the car announced, "You have arrived."

"I have?" I didn't see a house anywhere. "Oh, there's a driveway."

The cracked and buckled asphalt didn't inspire confidence as I turned in and maneuvered past bushy trees and towering shrubs. The driveway curved to the left, revealing a modest one-story ranch home. From what I could see, the backyard, or part of it, was enclosed in a chain-link fence with open land beyond. The lot had to be an acre or more, not that I knew about that sort of thing.

I pulled up next to an RV about three times the length of my car. On the right side of the driveway, in front of the garage, sat a four-door pickup truck and a boxy SUV with a few dents and more than a little rust.

Bobbie pulled something out of the tote bag that held our snacks.

"Are those brownies?" My mouth watered at the thought. "You've been holding out on me."

"They're not for you." She climbed out of the car, and Bernard and I followed her to the front steps.

Bernard rang the doorbell. "Remember, let me take the lead."

Taking in the peeling paint on the wood siding, I whispered, "With the house in foreclosure, I'm guessing they're not rolling in dough. That could work in our favor." My normally limited patience thinned as we waited for someone to answer the door. "Maybe you should knock."

"He's just lost his wife, and we know very little about his situation," Bernard said. "Let's try not to offend him right off the bat."

"Who me?"

The door swung open. A young woman, maybe mid-twenties, in a Pink Floyd T-shirt, leggings, and flip flops, shot us a glare from under a mop of dark unruly hair before fixing her gaze on the floor.

Bernard's warm smile could have melted an iceberg, but it had no effect on her. "We're here to see Mr. Vance. He's expecting us."

She turned her back to us and left us standing in front of the open door. I took a step to follow her, but Bernard held out his arm to block my way.

About a minute later, an unsmiling man appeared. He didn't look all that different from the fake Vance, except for a rounder face and gray stubble covering both his chins.

"My name is Bernard Fernsby." Bernard's smile softened, and he reached out a hand. "I'm so sorry to bother you at such a difficult time."

Vance shook Bernard's hand, muttering something under his breath, then invited us in. "Things are a bit messier than usual."

He walked with his shoulders slouched, as if tired of carrying the weight of the world on them. We followed him single file into a living room where the focal point was a fireplace surrounded by a brick wall. Cups and glasses cluttered the tables, along with a few beer bottles.

"I brought you some homemade brownies." Bobbie held them out to him, but when he stared at them blankly, she found an empty spot on the coffee table and set them down. He motioned to a beige leather sofa, and Bobbie and Bernard took their seats while he gathered up dirty dishes and carried them into the kitchen.

While waiting for Vance to return, I walked over to the sliding glass door that led to the fenced-in back yard. At least a dozen small dogs frolicked outside. A few lay sunning themselves, but most ran around chasing each other and play fighting.

When Vance returned, I asked, "Are those your stunt dogs?"

For the first time, he smiled. "They are." He came and stood next to me, pointing at a little white dog. "See the one who looks like a mop? That's Trixie. She's a character, but almost impossible to train. Audiences love her anyway, so I kept her. My wife loved her to pieces."

"I'm so sorry..."

He shook his head and stared out at the dogs. "You can't explain to a dog why their favorite human isn't around anymore." He sighed softly. "Not that I understand it much better."

The reality of his loss hit me, and at that moment, I regretted being there. To offer him money at a time like this seemed crass. I looked over at Bobbie and Bernard. "We shouldn't have come."

Vance gave my shoulder a fatherly pat. "It's fine, really. Any distraction is welcome, to be honest. And I was really happy to hear that Roxy is alive and well."

"Roxy? Oh right. We call her Kit, short for Kitsune.

That's Japanese for fox." I stopped myself from rambling. "She's better than well."

"And talk about a character," Bobbie said, joining in. "Everybody loves her. Especially Whit."

"That's me," I said, in case he wondered since Bernard hadn't gotten around to introducing us. "And that's my grandmother, Bobbie."

He tipped his ball cap. "Nice to meet you."

"We were hoping..." The words stuck in my throat, and I tried again. "That is, I was hoping that we could work something out so she could stay with me." Before he could answer, I added, "She's really happy living with us."

He stared out the window while I waited for his answer. "Can you believe she used to climb over that chain-link fence? Never seen anything like it. I had to keep her in her kennel most of the time to keep her from getting out."

The thought of Kit stuck in a cage made me like Vance less, but I didn't say anything. At that moment, I knew I wouldn't let him have her back. I'd figure something out if he didn't agree. I had to make sure she didn't spend another day or night in a cage.

"She's been with us for months." I searched for something I could say to convince him. "Don't you think she's been through enough? She belongs with us."

He didn't look at me. "It's not really my decision to make."

Chapter Thirteen

If letting us keep Kit wasn't up to Vance, then who?

I glanced at Bobbie before asking him, "Did you want to talk with your daughter about it? Or do you have a business partner?"

Before he answered, Bobbie came over to where we stood. "We'd love to invite you up to Arrow Springs to see how well Kit has adjusted."

He made his way to the recliner, sat down, and raised the footrest, exposing the soles of his work boots. Bobbie had taught me you could tell where people had been by inspecting the bottom of their shoes.

Vance's shoes told me he hadn't worn them outdoors since he'd bought them. Unless he cleaned the soles, but who does that?

"I can't leave the dogs. I'd ask Jan—my daughter—to hold down the fort, but..." His voice drifted off and he stared at his hands.

"I'm sure losing her mother has been very hard on her.

On both of you." Bobbie scooted forward in her seat and shoved herself to a standing position. "Why don't we come back and bring Kit to see you? How about one day next week?"

"I'm here every day." He brought his recliner to the fully erect position.

Even though Bobbie told him not to bother, he walked us outside. Bobbie and Bernard headed for the car while I strolled over to the truck on the other side of the driveway.

"That's a nice truck." I did my best to sound nonchalant. "I've been thinking about getting a four-wheel drive since I moved up to the mountains." I'd seen what I wanted, so I thanked Vance and got in the driver's seat.

Once everyone had buckled up, I put the car in reverse. "Is he looking at me suspiciously?"

Bobbie looked over at Vance and waved. "Hard to tell, but he's watching us like he wants to make sure we leave."

When we exited the driveway, Bernard leaned forward in his seat. "What was that all about?"

"Pine needles." I let that sink in for a moment. "In the tread of his tires."

⬦ ⟶

Bobbie insisted on stopping at her favorite behemoth membership store before driving home. "Drop me off by the entrance and pick me up in forty-five minutes."

"You don't want me to come with you?" I asked, disappointed.

Bobbie gave me a long-suffering look. "If you go with me, it will take two hours and cost at least twice as much."

Before she opened the door, she added, "And don't you two go solving the case without me."

"What about lunch?" I asked. Sometimes I thought the two of them would die of starvation if I weren't there to remind them to eat. "Want to go somewhere after you're done shopping?"

Bernard answered for her. "We'll want to get back up the mountain before dusk. The road will freeze up as soon as the sun goes down."

"Fine. But I'm getting something to eat. Do you want us to get you something?"

"Thank you, dear, but no. The snacks will hold me until dinner."

We drove around the area until I spotted a sign that said "Rosie's Diner." I pulled into a spot near the entrance.

"How's this look?" I asked.

The bell on the door jingled as we entered the old-fashioned restaurant. Wooden booths covered in red vinyl lined one side, with a counter running along the other side. The scent of coffee and freshly baked pies filled the air.

A middle-aged server with curly hair and a warm smile greeted us and showed us to a booth. Bernard ordered a cup of coffee while I perused the menu.

Taking a long sip of his black, dark-roast coffee, Bernard waited while I decided what to eat. When I finally looked up, he looked at me expectantly.

"You think Vance has been up to Arrow Springs, don't you?" he asked.

"I think the truck has. Vance doesn't seem like the type to murder someone, does he? I mean, his wife passing away doesn't exactly give him an alibi, but the timing seems weird. Maybe losing someone you loved made you go off the deep end. Or..." A thought popped into my head. "What if his wife was murdered?"

The waitress picked that moment to appear, and I hoped she hadn't overheard me. I ordered a BLT with crispy bacon and a mocha with extra whipped cream, and Bernard requested a burger and fries. When I got to be his age, I'd make sure to eat better.

As soon as the waitress stepped away from the table, Bernard shared more of what he'd learned. "Vance's wife died of natural causes after a long illness."

"What did you think of his daughter?" I wished we'd had spent more time with her and maybe asked her a few questions. "Maybe the sullen, sad recluse in mourning was all an act. Maybe she took the truck up to Arrow Springs to confront Guy Patro—"

"Pavlakovich."

"Right. Maybe she went to confront him, and things got out of hand." But why? Because she wanted Kit back? She didn't seem at all interested in us, our dog, or any of the dogs, for that matter.

Bernard interrupted my train of thought. "Lots of places have pine needles. Maybe there were pine trees at the funeral."

I pulled out my phone. "Do you know the name of the funeral home? They should have some pictures online. Or I can check out the street view on my maps app."

He chuckled. "You're turning into quite the detective, Whit. Have you thought of getting your license too? You know, Bobbie is trying to get me to sell her the agency, and

I'm seriously considering her offer. She could use you on the team."

"She wants to buy your business? But she's just an apprentice."

"I'll stay on at least until she gets her license."

I stabbed at my foamy mocha with my spoon. "*If* she gets her license. What if she loses interest? Then what? Or what if she breaks a hip or has a stroke? She's old, you know."

The way Bernard narrowed his eyes reminded me he was even older than Bobbie. The waitress brought our food, and we ate in silence, except for me asking if I could steal a few of Bernard's fries.

Once I'd polished off my sandwich, I laid a few bills on the counter to cover my part of the bill. "I need to take a walk before I get back in the car for the long drive home."

Bernard did not want to join me on my walk, so I left him to linger over his coffee and stepped out into the bright sunshine. It felt great to be in warm temperatures again. The nearby hardware store didn't appeal to me, at least not at the moment, so I headed in the opposite direction toward Wine and More.

On the way, I peeked in the windows of several clothing stores and drooled at the cute outfits on display. Sadly, I'd have to wait until I got a real job again before I spent money on anything other than essentials.

A creepy crawly tingle went up my spine. I glanced over my shoulder, but the only people nearby were a young couple walking and holding hands, completely focused on each other. I turned my attention to a car cruising the parking lot, and as soon as I did, the driver hit the gas pedal, revving the engine as it drove away.

Taking a note of the plate number, I opened the notes app on my phone and typed it in, hoping I got it right. I added a description of the car, though "late model gray sedan" could describe half the cars out there. I closed my eyes, trying to picture the logo—roundish and squiggly. That definitely wouldn't narrow things down, though at least I could report that it wasn't a Tesla. Or any other electric car from the sounds of it.

Was my imagination getting the better of me? Considering I'd found a dead body just a few days earlier, it made sense to be overcautious. A nagging question tugged at my brain.

Who would follow me? And why?

Chapter Fourteen

My phone buzzed with a call. I checked the screen, figuring I'd ignore it until I saw the caller was Jenna. My heart skipped a beat.

I answered with, "Is Kit okay?"

"She's fine," Jenna said. "But there's someone at the door and they won't go away. I don't like it."

"Don't open the door."

"I'm not going to." Jenna sighed loud enough for me to hear it. "Make them go away."

"I'll call someone to come over and we'll come back right now."

After texting Bobbie, I jogged back to the coffee shop. I soon hustled Bernard out of the diner, and we went to pick up Bobbie. We found her waiting in front of the store with several grocery bags.

"Who's at our door?" she asked as I put the bags in the trunk.

"That's what I'd like to know." I closed the trunk and

got back in the driver's seat. "Who can we call to go over and check? Rosa? Gypsy—I mean, Sunny?"

"Those old farts?" Bobbie's brow furrowed in concentration. "We should send someone who can handle themselves. I'll see if Elijah can go over."

"And I'll call Tess. For all I know, she's still with Elijah."

"What does that mean?"

I filled in on the two lovebirds and how, when I'd last seen them the previous evening, they'd been all over each other. Bobbie chuckled.

"What's funny about that?" I asked, but she didn't answer me. Maybe she'd realized I'd been interested in Elijah myself and was gloating, but that wasn't like her.

Ten minutes later, when we'd reached the turn for Arrow Springs, Tess called back. "It's a messenger with a letter. I tried to tell him I was you, but he wouldn't give it to me without showing him ID."

After sharing the information with Bobbie and Bernard, I relaxed and enjoyed the drive up the windy road. Soon, the scenery turned to pine trees and patches of white on the side of the road. The bright sunshine had melted most of the snow at the lower levels, but as the elevation increased, so did the thickness of the snowpack.

Bobbie nagged me to slow down. "You never know when you're going to hit a patch of ice," she warned. I reluctantly complied.

When I finally pulled the car into the driveway, I threw the gearshift into park and jumped out, leaving Bobbie and Bernard to fend for themselves. Tess, Elijah, and Henry stood next to a man in a heavy windbreaker and baseball cap with a logo.

"Hey, you guys." I greeted the messenger with, "Boy, you sure are persistent."

"Can I see your ID?"

"And focused, I see." I pulled out my license and showed it to him. He held out a clipboard and asked me to sign, then handed me a sealed envelope and walked to his van.

"What is it?" Tess asked.

As I ripped open the envelope and unfolded a document, my heart sank. "It's from Vance's lawyer. It says we have to return Kit by three PM tomorrow or they'll have me arrested." Frantically, I turned to Bobbie, not wanting to believe what it said.

"Let me see that." Bobbie reached for the letter and reviewed it before handing it to Bernard. "Mr. Vance didn't say anything about this when we were there. Do you think he'd already talked to his lawyer?"

"He must have." Bernard reviewed the letter. "Lawyers don't work that quickly in my experience."

"Jerk." A surge of anger coursed through me. "And here I was, all sympathetic. 'Sorry for your loss, Mr. Vance.' Meanwhile, he knew this would be waiting for us when we got home. Why didn't he tell us so when we were there?"

Bernard handed the notice back to. me. "I'm guessing he wanted to avoid a confrontation."

I stood amid the group, wishing they would all go away so I could break down and cry or yell or both.

Tess took my arm. "Why don't we go inside?"

"I'll make a pot of coffee." Bobbie unlocked the door and called out, "We're home, Jenna."

Jenna appeared, clutching Mr. Whiskers to her chest. "Oh, thank goodness." She gathered her things. "I'm going home now."

"You don't want to stay and have coffee?" Bobbie asked. "Or tea?"

"Oh, no." Jenna gave Bobbie a meek smile as she hurried to the door. "Mr. Whiskers and I need some quiet time after all the excitement."

The moment Jenna and her cat left, Kit squirmed out from under the sofa and ran first to me and then Henry, rubbing on his shoes. He took a seat on the sofa and Kit jumped into his lap, rolling over for him to rub her belly as she blissfully closed her eyes.

Bobbie's gaze went from Elijah to Tess, then lingered on Henry. "Coffee or tea? I could make both. It's no trouble."

"I need something stronger." I headed straight for the china cabinet where Bobbie kept the liquor.

My hands shook as I set bottles on the dining room table. Elijah hurried over. "Let me do that, Whit."

I turned to him and willed myself not to cry. "But I have to do something."

"Okay, we'll work together." He took stock of our alcohol inventory and seemed to mull over the options. "Do you have apple cider? And some lemons?"

"We always have lemons." I went into the kitchen and checked the refrigerator, returning with the bottle of cider.

"How does an apple cider margarita sound?" he asked. "You can warm the apple cider and I'll take care of the rest. And if anyone doesn't want alcohol, I'll make them a virgin version."

"What will that be?" I asked, happy for the distraction. "Apple cider and simple syrup?"

"And a squeeze of lemon."

Henry and Tess came over to the dining room table to watch Elijah work while I returned to the kitchen to heat the cider. Bobbie joined me.

"I'm hungry." It hadn't been that long since lunch, but food was comforting and that's what I needed at that moment.

"You're always hungry. Oh, to have the metabolism of a thirty-year-old."

"I'm only twenty-nine," I corrected her.

"Your cider is boiling over."

"Eek!" I pulled the pot off the stove and grabbed six mugs, filling them with hot cider. Bobbie gave me a tray to carry them to the dining room, where I found the others around the table, talking.

Bobbie brought out an oversized bowl of homemade snack mix and set it on the table. "I have a call to make." She disappeared down the hallway.

I squeezed between Tess and Henry at the dining table. Kit jumped on my lap, no doubt hoping to get on the table and snatch some snacks.

The drinks were the right combination of sweet and sour and warmed me from the inside. My mood didn't budge, remaining somewhere between anger at the world and desperation. While I stroked Kit's fur mindlessly, I tried to think about a plan that would allow Kit to stay with Bobbie and me.

We'd tried reasoning with Vance. What else could we do? While the others chatted about the weather and other inconsequential subjects, I revisited the idea of taking Kit and going into hiding. It seemed like a drastic solution, but I'd run out of other ideas.

Bobbie returned to the dining room and waved me over, leading me into the living room and away from the others.

"My lawyer says there's nothing we can do to avoid giving Kit back to Vance tomorrow. In the longer term, he has some ideas, but they're going to take some time. And unless we can come up with concrete evidence that she's being mistreated..."

A flood of emotions rose inside me—mostly anger and frustration. I wanted to lash out, but I knew Bobbie was on my side, so I shoved those feelings deep where all my other dark emotions lived.

My breath came in shallow gulps. "We have to do something, Bobbie."

Tess came over to my side. "I know you've gotten attached to her, Whit." She paused. "But she's just a dog."

"Just a dog?" I bellowed, ready to pick a fight with her right then and there. But Tess wasn't done talking.

"What happens when you go back to work?" she asked. "Let's face it, our jobs don't leave much time for taking care of a pet. Are you going to just dump her off with Bobbie?"

"I—" I began, but the truth was I hadn't given it that much thought.

I hadn't even noticed that Bobbie had left until she returned with a plate of brownies.

She held them out to Tess. "Maybe she's not going back to her job."

"Of course, I am." I grabbed a brownie and shoved half of it in my mouth before walking over to the fireplace and staring at the gray ashes.

The empty frame where Julia's picture had been mocked me with its blank white emptiness. It made me think of the hole inside me she left when she gave me up. Why did life have to be so complicated?

For some reason, Tess calling Kit "just a dog" stung. Funny thing, I might have made a similar comment before the little rascal showed up on my doorstep. Pets were fine for other people, but I didn't understand why people would take on the responsibility and expense until Kit came into my life.

It had taken a while for her to grow on me, but once she did, I couldn't imagine life without her.

Henry's soft voice broke through my thoughts. "Why don't we take Kit for a walk and talk about it?"

At her name, Kit scurried over to his side. With a glance over at Bobbie, I agreed, and went to the closet for my coat. Kit wiggled while I tried to clip the leash on.

"Would you just sit still?" I snapped.

Kit froze and whimpered, and she lay down on the floor, looking up at me like a child who'd just gotten scolded.

"I'm sorry, Kit," I whispered. "I'm not mad at you." I stroked her head and gave her chin a scratch the way she liked, then clipped the leash on her harness and opened the door.

The crisp, cold air shocked me, and I squinted in the

blazing sun. By the time I got used to the mountain winter, it would be spring. Kit wagged her tail while she hurried from shrub to shrub, sniffing intently as she chose the perfect spot to pee.

Henry's voice broke the silence. "Funny how the sun can be shining brightly, but it's still so cold."

I recognized his attempt to make small talk and get my mind off of the impending deadline, but it didn't work. We walked in silence down the driveway and down the street, Kit pulling me eagerly.

"You know," he began, his voice kind and soft, "if you want, I could take her to the owner. Vance, I think you said his name is? It might be easier on you, or at least not quite as hard as having to take her yourself."

I didn't answer right away. I didn't want anyone to take Kit away from me. Was I trying to deny the inevitable?

I finally spoke. "You don't understand. I can't give her back to Vance. Kit's got issues, and I don't think she was treated very well. How would you feel if you had to leave your happy home and go back to a place where every night, instead of snuggling in bed with someone who loved you, you had to sleep in a cage?"

"Kinda hard to say," he said. "I'm not a dog."

"Oh, so you agree with Tess? She's just a dog?"

"I didn't say that." Henry frowned.

But that's what you think was what I wanted to say. *That's what you all think.*

"She's more than a dog." I didn't have words to describe what she meant to me, how she'd found an opening in my armor and snuck into my heart the way no one else had done. There was only one way I could describe it. "She's family."

He nodded. "What are you planning to do?"

What could I do?

Kit chose that moment to look up and cock her head to one side as if she wanted to hear my answer too. "I'll think of something."

Chapter Fifteen

Kit. Vance. Kit. Vance.

I'd forgotten about everything else in my life. That one dog and that one man consumed my thoughts while I tried to come up with a plan to keep from losing Kit. I'd barely given my career a thought, not to mention the upcoming Christmas holidays, or even Julia, for that matter.

Or the murder.

The cops would solve the murder eventually, and it had little to do with me, even if Kit did know Guy Pavlakovich.

But what if...?

At that moment, I knew who the murderer had to be, even if I couldn't prove it. Yet. It had to be Vance.

"Hey!" I yelled at Henry, and Kit perked up her ears. "I've got it."

"Got what?" he called after me.

"A plan." I shoved the door open and rushed over to

the table where Bobbie, Bernard, Tess, and Elijah stared at me with wide eyes.

"Vance is the murderer," I announced.

Bobbie tilted her head to one side. "He's certainly one of the top suspects."

"No. You don't understand. He came up here in his four-wheel-drive truck and killed Pavo—" I started over. "Vance killed Guy, because he was about to double cross him."

"It's a good theory," Bernard began.

"It's not just a theory," I insisted. "And all we have to do is prove it by three o'clock tomorrow, and he'll go to jail. He can't take Kit from us if he's in jail, right?"

"Oh," Bobbie nodded, finally understanding. "That's an excellent point."

"What about the daughter?" Bernard asked. "Wouldn't she take control of her father's assets, including Kit?"

"She didn't seem at all interested in the dogs to me. I bet we can offer her a few hundred bucks and she'll let us keep Kit."

"You might be right about that," Bobbie agreed. "How do we prove Vance murdered Pavlakovich?"

"We start by placing Vance in town the day of the murder," I said. "Bernard? Any ideas on how to do that?"

Bernard pursed his lips, nodding his head before speaking. "I can check with my contact on the force and see if I can review the traffic cam footage for earlier that day. Maybe I'll get lucky and spot the truck. I don't remember seeing security cameras in front of the inn, and

I'm pretty good at noticing those things. But there might be a camera next door or across the street."

"And ask if they found his pinky ring in his room. I saw him wearing it earlier. I'm thinking Vance might have taken it to make it look like a robbery gone bad."

"That's a good point." Bernard smiled as if proud of his newest protégée.

"I'll go into town and see what I can find out. Maybe someone saw him or his truck. Do we have a picture of him?"

"Try the Stunt Dog's Extravaganza's website," Bernard suggested.

I typed the site into my phone's browser, then clicked through the menu until I came to the "About Us" page where I found a picture of a smiling Jonathan Vance. It was a few years old, but it would do.

"I'll go with you," Henry said.

"Thanks, but this is something I need to do on my own. If I'm by myself, I might get someone to open up and tell me something they didn't mention to the police or maybe something they'd forgot or didn't think was important at the time."

Before I even opened the closet door to get my jacket, Kit ran to the door and pranced happily back and forth as if she meant to keep me from leaving without her.

"Okay, girl. You can come with. Help me sniff out the clues."

⊰ ⇢ ⊱

Elijah offered me a ride into town, but I turned him down. A walk would give me some time to think. I stood stiffly while Tess gave me a hug. She and Henry got in the car, and I watched them drive away.

Kit pulled on the leash, eager to go for her walk. She had no idea that we might soon be separated forever. What would she think if I could ask her? She might have enjoyed being around all the other dogs, but I knew she would hate being locked in a cage.

As I made my way down the hill, my boots sank into the soft, muddy ground. Most of the snow had melted, leaving only small patches of white scattered here and there. A breeze ruffled through the trees, whispering softly while the branches swayed gently.

I stepped carefully, doing my best to avoid the slick spots. Sliding down a hill of mud wouldn't be nearly as much fun as on the snow and even more embarrassing. Kit pranced through the muck, happy to be out of the house.

The sun had dipped behind the mountains and the streetlights came on at once. My first stop was the Arrow Springs Inn.

As I entered, I slipped out of my jacket, shoving my knit hat and gloves into various pockets. My hopes dimmed at the sight of a woman standing behind the front desk. I'd planned to question Gary further, but maybe his coworker knew a thing or two. I greeted her and learned that Gary's shift would begin at six that evening.

Keeping my voice down so others wouldn't overhear, I proceeded carefully. "I suppose you've heard about the murder the other night."

With an exasperated sigh, she exclaimed, "Oh. My.

God. That's all anyone can talk about. And the questions! 'Is it safe here?' 'Has the murderer been caught?' and my favorite, 'Is the murderer a guest in the hotel?' How the heck should I know?"

"That must be exhausting," I commiserated. "There must be a lot of gossip, too. Does anyone talk about what they saw or who might have killed him?"

"Only about some woman they saw running down the stairs around that time. She was chasing a little dog..." Her eyes widened, and she leaned over the counter and glimpsed Kit wagging her tail. "That was you?"

"Yeah, that was me. But I didn't murder him, in case you were wondering. I did find the body, though."

She grimaced. "I'm just glad I wasn't on shift." She lowered her voice to a whisper. "Gary said he saw the dead guy."

"And promptly passed out."

Covering her mouth to hide her snicker, she said, "Excuse me," and went into the office, closing the door behind her. I could hear her laughing through the door.

She returned to her post a minute or so later, wiping her eyes. "It's just so sad."

I nodded in sympathy, although I knew those were tears of laughter, not sadness. I figured it would be rude to put her on the spot.

"Besides me and my dog, has anyone mentioned seeing someone going up or down the stairs around that time? Or anything else unusual or out of place?"

"Let me think." Her eyes wandered around the room. "More than one man has mentioned an attractive, dark-haired woman they saw earlier that day. Oh, but maybe that was you."

On a whim, I pulled out Julia's picture even though her hair wasn't dark. "Was it this woman?"

She looked at the photo, then handed it back to me. "Never seen her."

I was ready to give up when I remembered Vance's picture. Holding my phone out for her to see, I asked if she recognized him.

"Doesn't look familiar at all. But he has that sort of forgettable face, don't you think?"

I took a second look and had to admit she had a point. Still, I might as well show the people in the lobby the picture and maybe some of the staff.

"Do you know who was at work that evening besides Gary?"

She shook her head. "We don't have a big staff. At that time of the day, the only people working are the restaurant staff and the front desk clerk. The maids are long gone by then."

"You handle everything that goes on here? Checking people in? Getting them extra towels?"

"Pretty much."

"Wow." Having a hospitality job sounded like a lot of work. "What if a toilet overflows or something like that?"

"If I can't handle it, I call a plumber."

"I see." That seemed like a lot of responsibility for one person. "Whatever they're paying you, it's not enough."

"You got that right."

I doubted the restaurant staff would have seen people coming and going, and I didn't think Vance had stopped to eat before or after the murder. But I wanted to be thorough.

The host saw me and hurried over. "I'm so sorry, no dogs allowed."

"That's okay. I just wondered if you or any of your staff saw anything when the dead guy was found."

"I heard all the commotion and came out to the lobby to see what was going on." He narrowed his eyes. "Wasn't that you who the police questioned?"

"I found the body."

"Then you saw a lot more than I did. Gary came over and told us all to get back to work."

I thanked him for his time and returned to the lobby. Kit tugged on the leash. Figuring she smelled food, I let her lead me to the sofa by the fireplace.

"Henry?" I shouldn't have been surprised to run into him again since he was staying at the inn.

"Hi, Whit." He reached down to scratch Kit behind her ears.

"Careful," I warned. "Her paws got pretty muddy on the way over. I'll get something to wipe them down with."

Kit seemed content to stay where she was, so I stepped into the ladies' room and wet down a few paper towels. By the time I returned, Kit lay belly-up in Henry's lap.

I wiped the mud off her paws. "She usually doesn't take to men, but she sure likes you. Do you walk around with beef jerky in your pocket?"

He laughed. "Always. Just in case." His smile faded, and he lowered his voice. "Are you serious about going around asking questions? Don't you think that's... I don't know... dangerous?"

I perched on the edge of the chair next to him. "I have to do something before they take Kit away from me. If I can prove Vance is a murderer, he'll go to jail for a really long time and Kit can stay with me."

"Interesting plan. How do you plan to prove it?"

I slumped back in the chair. "All I've got so far is pine needles in the tread of his tires, and that's not even enough to get the police to investigate further. If they searched his house, they might find his pinky ring."

"Pinky ring?" His eyebrows rose in question.

"Yeah. Guy was wearing it when I came to see him, but when I came back and found his body later, it was gone. It was less than an hour later, so I doubt he stashed it away somewhere. But Bernard is going to check with the police to see if they found it."

"If they found the pinky ring in Vance's possession, that would certainly be incriminating. Do you think it would be enough to charge him with murder?"

I sighed. "I don't know. That's why I'm asking around town. If someone saw him or his truck that day, then that should be enough to at least get a search warrant for his home. He claimed he was home, but I think he scrubbed the soles of his boots clean. He didn't think to check his tire treads, though. Eagle eyes, that's me, spotted the pine needles." I looked around the room. "I'm going to talk to a few more people here, then I'm off to the General Store."

"Want me to come with you?"

His eyes, warm and comforting, almost made me say yes. But I didn't need any distractions while on my mission to find the truth.

I questioned a middle-aged couple dressed in high-quality natural fibers in neutral tones who sat drinking wine by the window. They remembered seeing me chasing Kit through the lobby and not much else. The woman pointed at Henry and said she remembered him but didn't recall what day. No doubt every woman with a pulse and some of the men noticed him. I asked about the dark-haired woman, but that seemed to spark a potential argument, so I moved on.

I spoke briefly with a gray-haired man waiting for his wife to come down from their room. They'd just driven up from Bakersfield that day and hadn't heard about the murder until I mentioned it. Our conversation got awkward quickly, so I excused myself and left. I'd come back later to talk to Gary and see if there were more guests to question.

Bundling up against the cold before stepping outside, I missed being able to go out in December wearing a T-shirt and flip flops. What else did I miss about L.A.? I couldn't think of anything at that moment, but I had other things on my mind.

Arrow Springs had started to feel like home in a way that felt new, and I liked the feeling. I promised myself I'd come up and visit Bobbie more often once I got back to work.

At the entrance to the General Store, I hesitated, then picked Kit up and tucked her under my jacket. What Scooter didn't know wouldn't hurt him. I found him stocking the candy display next to the register.

"Hey, Scooter."

He straightened with a jerk, spilling candy bars onto the floor, then bent down to pick them up.

"Sorry." I gave him an apologetic smile. "Didn't mean to startle you."

He mumbled a reply, but I couldn't make out the words.

"What's that?"

He cleared his throat and repeated, "No dogs allowed."

"How'd you—?" Before I finished my question, I noticed Kit's tail peeking out from the bottom of my jacket. "I just wanted to ask you something, then we'll leave."

He picked up the last candy bar and returned to his position behind the counter.

"Do you happen to remember seeing this guy a few days ago? Maybe he came into the store?"

Scooter frowned at the picture, then shrugged.

"You didn't see him?" I asked. "Or you're not sure?"

He grabbed a cloth and wiped down the counter in wide circles. "A lot of people come in here, you know. Locals, tourists, lots of people."

"Of course. I just thought maybe someone saw him. You know about the man who was murdered at the inn, right? I think this man is the murderer." I pointed to the picture displayed on my phone, and he glanced at it again briefly before straightening a chapstick display. "I'm trying to find someone who saw him."

"Oh." Scooter paused, then turned his attention to a tiered tower of cigarette lighters, rearranging them by color. "Too bad you can't look at the security camera footage."

"You have a security camera? Where? Out front?"

When he nodded, I asked, "What do you mean too bad I can't look at the footage? Why not?"

"Can't," he said. "Not without a warrant. That's what my boss said."

Darn it. I considered trying to talk him into showing it to me, but Scooter was a stickler for the rules. "Okay, see you."

I stepped onto the sidewalk, blinking in the bright sunshine, and sent Bernard a text. He might know if other businesses on the main street had security cameras. Would anyone let me look at their footage without a warrant?

A sense of hopelessness washed over me and an emptiness tugged at the pit of my stomach. It might mean a lot of things, but I knew a quick fix—a cinnamon roll from Sugarbuns Bakery.

Chapter Sixteen

I let Kit walk even though that meant the two-minute walk took twenty minutes. It gave me time to think.

The aroma of cinnamon and vanilla filled my nostrils the moment I stepped inside Sugarbuns. The woman who'd been working on my last visit looked up and greeted me with, "Oh, hey."

"Hey." I glanced at her name tag, figuring I might as well know her name before I grilled her. I'd never met anyone under a hundred named Mitsy, but that's what it said. "Since it looks like I'm going to be a regular, thanks to your cinnamon rolls, I might as well introduce myself. I'm Whit. And you already know Kit's name, I think."

She came around the counter and crouched down to Kit's level. "How's my little snuggly wuggly? Did you know you got me in trouble the other day?" She looked up at me. "My boyfriend made me change my shirt and take a shower as soon as I got home. It was totally worth it."

"Mitsy's an interesting name," I said.

"I was named after my grandmother. I hated it when I was a kid, but now I like it. It's unique, you know?"

While she was occupied giving Kit attention, I jumped into my questions. "Do you guys have security cameras?" She'd been so friendly, I hoped she might let me see the footage.

"Nah, my boss doesn't think it's worth getting one. We hardly have any cash on hand, and who would want to steal a bunch of pastries?"

When I raised my hand, she laughed.

My optimism slipping away, I showed her a picture of Vance. "Have you seen him?"

"Nope."

"You sound very confident."

"I never forget a face."

"Is that so?" I tucked that information away for potential future use. I hadn't really expected Vance to stop in for coffee and a pastry either before or after murdering Guy, but I still felt disappointed at finding one more person who hadn't seen Vance.

Still, I only needed to find one person who'd noticed him the day of the murder. But what if he'd worn some sort of disguise? Or more likely, he'd worn a hat and scarf covering half his face. With our frigid temperatures, he'd fit right in.

"Has anyone said anything about the murder the other day at the inn?" I asked.

"Oh, sure. Like, 'can you believe it?' and stuff like that."

"Anyone asking questions? Besides me, that is."

"Not about the murder," she said. "But there's this one

guy who asked me about you. I think he has a crush on you. He has these really light blue eyes."

"Henry?"

"He didn't say his name."

I pulled out my phone and scrolled to the picture Tess had taken of Henry and me. "Is this him?"

"Yeah. Pretty hot for an old guy."

"Old guy? He can't be more than late thirties."

She shrugged, and I wondered if she thought I was old. I'd be turning thirty in a few months. I turned to go.

"Aren't you forgetting something?" she asked.

"Oh, right." I must have been seriously preoccupied to forget about the cinnamon rolls. Not sure how many people would be waiting for me at home, I ordered a half dozen. "And a triple latte. I'm not planning to sleep until I solve this murder and make sure that Kit can stay with me."

She stopped in the middle of bagging the rolls. "What's Kit got to do with the murder?"

"Maybe nothing. But also maybe everything."

◆ ◈ ◆

As I stepped outside, I turned toward the inn and contemplated where to stop and eat my cinnamon roll. I heard footsteps behind me. The source a pair or women's high-heeled boots if I wasn't mistaken, but why would Tess be following me?

I stopped in front of the souvenir shop and pretended to peer inside as I checked out the woman not far behind me. It wasn't Tess, but I was right about the high-heeled boots. The petite woman, carrying several shopping bags, had stopped in front of Toppers and appeared to focus on the hats in the window. She wasn't fooling me.

As I approached her, she turned toward me, smiling slightly. Exuding confidence in a designer puffer coat and fur-trimmed hat, she watched intently as I scoped her out. She was barely my height with her three-inch heels.

Her smooth olive skin, slightly darker than mine, practically glowed, but that was probably the expensive skin care products and makeup she used.

I figured I'd try the direct approach. "Why are you following me?" I wanted to add, "you little shrimp," but figured I'd start out being nice and save the insults for later.

Her eyes widened ever so slightly, and she spoke with a slight accent. "Why would I be following you?"

"Yes, exactly. That's my question."

"Have we met?" Her smile widened. "I'm Isabella Barrera." She reached out a leather-gloved hand, which I ignored.

"You're not from around here, are you?" I asked.

"I'm not." She turned back to the hat shop window. "Perhaps I'll get a cowboy hat for my father. I think he would like that. What do you think?"

"That's a Spanish accent, isn't it?" I tried to place the accent geographically. "But you're not Mexican. And not Spanish from Spain."

"Such a bright, young lady. I'm from South America. I'm here on an errand, hoping to return with a surprise for my father."

"It's a long way to come for a cowboy hat," I said, tiring of her non sequiturs. "Pretty sure they sell them online."

"Yes, I'm sure they do, but the hat is not what I meant by a surprise. I am hoping to surprise him with a person. His granddaughter."

I blinked and stared at her, waiting for her to continue, but she appeared to be waiting for me to make the next move. "Okay, this is fascinating, but I would like to circle back to my original question. Why are you following me?"

She didn't answer right away. "I would think a bright, young lady like yourself could figure it out." A smile spread across her lips. "Did you happen to notice that we look a little alike?"

I held my breath as I took in her words, then asked, "Are you saying we're related?"

Her smile masked whatever feelings she hid. "Very good. I knew you could figure it out. I believe you've never met your father or his family. Such a shame, don't you agree?"

I stared at her smooth, unlined face, but that meant little these days, especially with her olive complexion. She might be forty or fifty—Julia's age.

If this woman was my aunt, then her father would be... my grandfather? Was I the granddaughter she hoped to surprise him with?

After a long silence, I spoke. "You're my aunt?"

The smug look on her face annoyed me, but also told me I was right. This woman was my father's sister.

"Is there somewhere we can talk?" she asked.

"This really isn't a good time," I said. I'd gone my whole life never meeting my father or his family. They hadn't cared enough to get in touch until now, and they could wait another day or two. I wasn't turning my back on Kit when she most needed me.

Her eyebrows rose. "I thought you'd be curious and want to learn about your father."

"I'm free next week." I bristled at her manipulative tactics. "How about lunch on Tuesday?"

She shook her head. "I'm flying home before then. I hoped you would come with me. Your grandfather will be overjoyed when I arrive with you."

"Home?"

She hesitated, then said, "San Diego. I haven't told him I've found you. I want it to be a surprise. I only just learned that Julia," she said the "J" with an "H" sound, "and Alejandro had a baby. If my father had known sooner, he would have moved heaven and earth to find you."

Doing my best not to react to this news, I waited for her to continue. *My father's name is Alejandro.* No one in my family had ever shared that information. I'd never even seen a picture of him until I'd found the locket in the pawn shop.

In the back of my mind, a thought resurfaced. Bobbie claimed that my grandfather, Isabella's father, wasn't a good person. But she'd never gone into any details. And here stood my aunt, painting him as a genial family man.

"Why did you steal Julia's locket?" I asked. "And why sell it at the pawn shop? You obviously don't need money." Her clothes alone told me that.

"Do you mean this locket?" She reached into her pocket and pulled it out. "I had... borrowed it from Julia a while back, and I've kept it in my possession ever since. It helped me put two and two together and finally allowed me to locate you here. But the chain broke, and I lost it. What a relief to find it again."

I wasn't sure if I believed her, but I had no reason not to. Something told me Isabella really was my aunt, but that didn't mean I could trust her. I'd met plenty of people who were only out for themselves. If she wanted to reunite me with her father—my grandfather—then she had an ulterior motive.

She held out the locket. "Here. Take it." As if sensing my distrust, she added, "As a token of my sincerity. I will be leaving tomorrow for San Diego. I hope you will join me."

I held out my hand, palm up, willing it not to shake. She placed the oval locket on my palm, and I wrapped my fingers around it, feeling the cold metal against my skin.

Chapter Seventeen

After giving me her number, Isabella turned and walked away. I watched her until she rounded the corner, then pushed her out of my mind. Or at least I tried to. Conflicting emotions swirled in my body like a cyclone.

Returning my focus to the one person I still believed I could trust, I sent Bobbie a text. When she didn't answer, I sent one to Bernard. After several minutes with no answer, I called Bobbie's phone. She picked up on the first ring.

"Didn't you see my text?" I asked.

"This phone makes so many noises. How am I supposed to know what they all mean? I figured if something is important, I'll get a call. And I did."

I sighed. "Where are you?"

"We're at the police station. Where are you?"

"I just left the bakery with a half dozen cinnamon rolls. Why are you guys at the police station?"

"Let's meet up and we'll explain. Le Bon Chocolate," she said in a heavy French accent. "Give us about fifteen minutes and we'll meet you there."

"You know I don't speak French. But did you say chocolate?"

"I did. It's on the square two doors down from the General Store. It's tucked back in an alcove behind a candle shop and the herbalist, which is probably why you didn't notice it. Best hot chocolate in town, and they have a patio area. We can meet you there in fifteen minutes or so."

The patio area meant I didn't have to sneak Kit in under my coat. Which was good, since I hadn't fooled anyone that way.

Before meeting up with Bobbie and Bernard, I swung by Security Plus, curious if I was on Kelvin's bad side after the incident at Gypsy's the previous night. The lights were off, and I peered through the windows, looking for signs of life. Inside, the shadows seemed to move eerily, and I stepped back, nearly tripping over Kit.

"Let's go." I tugged her away from a fire hydrant just as the lights came on in the shop. As I waited, I heard footsteps inside, then the sound of the door unlocking.

Kelvin held the door open for Kit and me. "Sorry, I keep the front door locked when I'm working in the shop. Next time, you should knock."

"What do you do back there, anyway?" I asked. "Building a robot army to take over the world?"

He blinked before answering. "No. Of course not."

"I brought you a cinnamon roll." It seemed a good

excuse and better than starting off with asking for a favor. "From Sugarbuns. To make up for last night. Not that a pastry can make up for..." I stopped before saying the wrong thing and held it out to him. "Here."

"I'm on a high-protein diet." He smiled shyly. "My dad thinks if I bulk up a bit that I might..." He seemed to think he'd said too much.

"What? Get chicks? Don't you want to meet someone who will love you for who you are? There are plenty of guys with muscles that don't have half your brains."

"No, it's not that."

"Oh, well, okay. Let me know if you ever want to go to the gym. I haven't been in a week, and I feel like I'm losing my edge. I need to be strong and spry for my job."

"To mix drinks?"

I deflated. "I'm a stunt performer. You know, for the studios." When he gave me a blank look in return, I felt like I'd been challenged. "Watch this."

Quickly taking stock of the room, I bent at the knees and launched myself into the air, feeling weightless as I flipped backwards. My feet connected with the ground with a thud as I landed firmly, holding my arms out to my sides.

"Ta da." I waited for him to express how impressed he was.

"Now I remember," he said. "You used to be a gymnast. Weren't you supposed to go to the Olympics a few years ago?"

"Yeah. That's ancient history." I got to my other reason for stopping in. Taking Julia's locket out of my pocket, I handed it to him. "Can you tell me if there's a tracker in there?"

He raised one eyebrow. "You think you're being tracked?"

"Or maybe the former owner. Can you check?"

"Sure, but I can tell just by looking at it." He opened the locket but didn't comment on the two pictures inside. "There isn't a geotracking unit made that's small enough to fit inside."

"What about a bug? I'd feel better if you'd check with your whatchamacallit thingy."

He stepped away and returned with the wand. After turning it on and scanning the locket, he confirmed the absence of any tracking capabilities or listening devices.

"Thanks." After helping me out, it seemed only fair for me to buy something from him, but my budget was as tight as the faux leather skirt that no longer fit over my hips. I pulled a few bills from my pocket that I'd stashed there on my last bartending shift. "What kind of bug can I get for twenty bucks?"

He showed me a few items, and after some discussion, I picked out a tracker to attach to Kit's collar. That way, the next time she got out, I'd be able to find her.

Thanking Kelvin again, I hurried off to meet up with Bobbie and Bernard.

Behind the candle shop and herbalist, a low picket fence surrounded a wooden deck where I found Bernard. He sat at a table in the corner with his arms wrapped around himself and a scarf hiding half his face. I stepped through the gate and latched it behind me.

I dragged Kit over to the table. "It really cools off once the sun goes behind the mountains, doesn't it?"

He scowled in response. "Bobbie's inside getting the drinks."

Kit was itching to explore, so I let her off her leash and positioned myself with a view of the gate. I didn't expect her to try running away from me, but I didn't want to take any chances.

I jumped up when Bobbie appeared with a tray of mugs and hurried to open the gate and let her in. Bernard eyed the drinks eagerly, wrapping his hands around the paper cup as soon as she set his down.

"Mmmm. Whipped cream." I sipped the hot chocolate through the thick layer of cream and closed my eyes, savoring the rich taste. While I could have lingered in the patio, possibly going back for seconds, I was afraid Bernard might get frostbite if we stayed too long.

I pulled out my phone and opened the app where I'd made my notes. "I'll go first—it'll be quick. No one I talked to at the inn, the General Store, or Sugarbuns recognized Vance. Oh, that reminds me, speaking of Sugarbuns, anyone want a cinnamon roll along with their hot chocolate?" I held up the bag of still-warm pastries.

Bernard appeared to be torn, but he shook his head.

"You can take yours to go," I assured him, going back to my notes. "A few people, men mostly, mentioned a dark-haired woman who wasn't me. Actually, more than a few mentioned a dark-haired woman who *was* me, but I cleared that up pretty quickly."

Bobbie seemed interested. "At the inn?"

My mouth dropped open, and I shut it quickly, hoping

Bobbie didn't notice. Was the dark-haired woman Isabella?

"Whit?" Bobbie's voice brought me back to our conversation. "What about this mystery woman?"

"She was seen at the inn around the time of the murder."

"Hmph." Bernard stared at his hot chocolate, a bit of whipped cream on his upper lip.

Bobbie handed him a napkin. "What is it?"

"Could it have been Pavlakovich's accomplice?" Bernard asked, wiping his mouth. "The woman who claimed to be Mrs. Vance?"

I nearly spit out hot chocolate on the table. "That old bag?"

"Whit!" Bobbie scolded.

"Sorry. But I got the impression that the woman at the inn was hot or at least medium-warm. And the fake Mrs. Vance..." As I pictured her in my mind, I started to put the pieces in place. "Oh..." I didn't feel as smart as I had when I'd woken up that morning.

"What is it?" Bobbie's voice conveyed concern.

"The wig! She was wearing a wig. And about five layers of cheap fleece that made her look lumpy and probably much heavier than she really was."

"And those orthopedic shoes." Bobbie shook her head slowly. "Now that I think of it, I saw some just like them at the General Store."

Another memory popped into my head. "Along with the sale items in the back, including some left over from Halloween. I bet she found a wig there. It might have given her the idea to dress up and impersonate Mrs. Vance to claim Kit."

"So she's the one who killed Guy," Bobbie said.

I felt my chest tighten and forced myself to breathe. "No, it has to be Vance. It has to be." I stood and paced the length of the patio and back several times. Kit walked alongside me, dancing around my feet like we were playing some sort of game.

I returned to the table and stood next to my chair. "I don't want to solve the murder if it's not Vance. Is that terrible of me?"

Bobbie patted the seat until I sat back down. "Of course not, sweetie. You're don't want to lose Kit, and this feels like your last hope. But it's not."

Kit jumped onto my lap, and I tucked her under my jacket to keep her warm.

"Are you sure?" I asked.

"We're not done yet," Bernard said. "Just because there's a second suspect doesn't mean that Vance isn't guilty. And besides, this ultimatum from his lawyer may just be a negotiation tactic to get more money for Kit."

I brightened. "That makes sense. Thanks." I realized they hadn't filled me in on their progress with the police and the traffic cams. "What did you guys find out?"

One look told me they'd made little or no progress.

"My contact in the force is not on best terms with Wallenthorp, who is playing this close to the vest. I offered my help to review the traffic cam footage, but he turned me down. At least he appreciated learning about the missing pinky ring. I got the feeling he knew nothing about a ring, so I suspect they didn't find it in the room."

"But the killer might have taken it to throw the police off the track," Bobbie said. "Like a red herring."

"A red herring like in one of your whodunnits?" I asked, adding, "What a funny term."

"It's thought to have originated from the practice of using smelly fish—such as a red herring—to distract hounds from a scent they were tracking. The scent of the fish would throw off the dogs, just as the stolen ring might throw us off the trail of the murderer."

"Got it." Where did Bobbie come up with all this information?

"And unless the killer has no common sense," she continued, "they tossed it in a dumpster somewhere. Even if we found it, I doubt it would help identify the killer."

Bernard's ringtone played the Pink Panther theme song, and he stepped away from the table to answer his phone.

I felt emotionally drained and wanted nothing more than to curl up in front of the fire at home. Instead, I slurped the last of my hot chocolate and checked the time.

"Gary should be at the inn by now. Maybe he'll recognize Vance."

Bernard returned to the table. "Good news, or at least I hope it's good news. The police chief found out I'd offered to help review surveillance footage, and he's insisting that Wallenthorp accept my offer."

"You don't look that happy about it," I said. "Not looking forward to staring at a screen for hours?"

"It's not that." Bernard frowned. "I'd hoped to get on Wallenthorp's good side in the not-too-distant future, and now that seems unlikely."

"Maybe they'll fire him," I said cheerfully. "Then you can start fresh with the new guy."

Bernard chuckled. "You really are a glass-half-full kind of gal, aren't you?"

"That's me." I stood, ready to head off to the inn. "Sunshine and lollipops."

Chapter Eighteen

I hooked Kit back up to her leash. "See you guys later."

"Why don't you go with Whit?" Bernard suggested to Bobbie. "Two heads are better than one."

"That's what they say." Bobbie looked at me expectantly. "And we can cover twice as much ground."

It was a short walk back to the inn, which had begun to feel like a second home. Bobbie and I walked straight to the front desk, which sat empty. Aromas of garlic, onions, and other unidentified delicious scents wafted over from the dining room, reminding me it was dinnertime.

Bobbie rang the bell impatiently.

"Gary's probably getting someone extra towels or unclogging a toilet," I said, picking up a flyer for the upcoming Winter Wonderland and Craft Fair held annually at the park in the center of town.

"What are you talking about?" Bobbie asked.

"The front desk people have to do practically everything around here. And I bet they don't get paid much." A thought occurred to me. "I wonder if Gary had to clean the room after the crime scene people left. The maids only work day shifts."

I glanced around as Gary appeared at the top of the steps. He seemed about to run in the opposite direction until he caught me watching him. He ambled down the stairs, in no hurry to talk to us, which seemed suspicious. Of course, when you're looking for a murderer, almost everything seems suspicious.

"Hello, again," Bobbie said as he returned to his post behind the desk. "I don't think we were properly introduced the other evening. I'm Roberta Leland, but you can call me Bobbie. Everyone does. And this is my granddaughter, Whit."

Gary narrowed his eyes at me. "We've met."

"Hey, Gary." I leaned on the counter and lowered my voice. "You didn't happen to see a pinky ring in the dead guy's room, did you?"

He sputtered, caught off guard by my question. "I have no idea what you're talking about."

"Look, dude. I don't care if you happened to find it in a drawer..." no reaction, "or in the bathroom..." no reaction, "or maybe... under the bed?" His eyes widened every so slightly. "See, Gary, the police know about the missing pinky ring, and I wouldn't want them to find out that you're the one who took it. They might think *you* killed the guy in room 281."

"How do you know about—" Gary seemed to realize he should stop talking, so he did.

"Look, Gary. I know you didn't kill Patranovik."

"Pavlakovich," Bobbie corrected.

"Yeah, him." On the far wall, a shelf held a few potted plants and something that looked a lot like one of Kelvin's surveillance cameras. "I'm willing to keep quiet about the ring, though you might want to come up with a story for the police before they start asking questions. All I want in return is a quick look at the security footage."

"I don't know what you're talking about." He avoided eye contact, instead saying hello to a guest passing by.

I pointed to the potted plants. "My guess is there've been some issues with theft, so the management had cameras installed. They probably didn't tell you about them, but they didn't have to, did they? You weren't born yesterday, after all."

Gary cursed under his breath. "Those a-holes thought I wouldn't notice."

"Where is the footage stored?" I asked. "In the office?" When he didn't answer, I guessed again. "Online?"

He checked over his shoulder as if to make sure no one had snuck up behind him. "You won't tell anyone about... about any missing items?"

"You have my word."

Gary tore a sheet off a notepad and jotted down a website. "Here's the login and password."

"You've been very helpful." I gave Gary a warm smile and turned to Bobbie. "I think our work here is done."

When we arrived home, Bobbie put something in a pot to warm up and I turned on the laptop. I logged into the website and clicked an icon showing the date of the murder. A time stamp on the bottom of the screen allowed me to fast forward until I saw myself enter the frame.

There was no sound, but I could almost read my lips as I told Gary I wanted to see Jonathan Vance.

The camera was pointed at Gary's back, obviously intended to catch anyone working the front desk doing something sketchy, like cloning credit cards or accepting money from guests for an upgrade. I watched myself take a few steps away and disappear from the screen. The camera didn't capture me chasing after Kit, but I could tell by Gary's surprised, then amused expression when that had happened.

The murder occurred sometime between the time I left chasing after Kit and returned without her. I watched intently, barely daring to blink. My heart nearly stopped beating when I recognized the man who stepped up to the front desk.

Henry seemed cool and composed, then he walked off toward the front door. But where had he come from? I'd have to go back and see if there were any shots of him from earlier in the day.

Next, Gary left the front desk, though I couldn't tell what direction he went. Had he told the truth when he said he'd been called upstairs by a guest to help with their TV remote?

And then I saw her—the mystery woman with the long, wavy dark brown hair. She wore glasses with a Chanel logo—probably fake. Her heavy makeup accentuated high cheekbones and plump lips. The quality of the black and white recording didn't allow me to see much else, but with her low-cut sweater, I did get a good look at her boobs prominently displayed. No wonder all the men remembered seeing her.

She turned her head away from the camera as she passed the desk, and then she was out of range. I backed up several seconds and watched her walk by again. I stopped at the spot where the camera had the best view of her.

After noting the timestamp, I resumed watching. Less than ten minutes later I recognized myself walk past on my way to the stairs where I was about to discover Guy's dead body.

Bobbie came up behind me. "Find anything?"

I rewound the video to the timestamp where the mystery woman appeared. "Recognize her?"

Bobbie stared at the screen. "Why do young women feel the need to wear so much makeup? I bet she's a very pretty girl, but you can hardly tell. Like your friend Tess…"

I turned around to stare at her. "Really?"

"You're right. That's not important right now." She took a closer look. "I don't think I've seen her before."

"Are you sure?" I asked. "I get the feeling I've seen her somewhere…"

"You have been hanging around the inn quite a bit lately. Maybe you ran into her there. Or in town, like at the general store or the bakery."

"I think I would have remembered. She's not exactly someone who'd fade into the background."

"No," Bobbie agreed. "But picture her with a coat, hat and scarf, and she'd blend right in."

"That's just what I was thinking about Vance." I slumped in my chair. "I really, really hoped he would be on the footage. There's absolutely no evidence that he was in town that day. I'm still convinced he was here and killed Guy, but of course he wouldn't go walking around town introducing himself to everyone."

"Maybe Bernard will have better luck."

Bobbie's phone rang, and she showed me Bernard Fernsby's name on the display before she answered. There was "uh-huh" and "mmm" and other noncommittal syllables until she said, "Yes, I understand. You can only stare at a screen for so long. You'd risk missing something and then you'd have to start all over."

Bobbie ended the call, but I didn't need her to tell me he hadn't yet seen Vance's truck on the traffic cam.

The thing that Bobbie had warmed up on the stove turned out to be leftover beef stroganoff, and when I wasn't paying attention, she'd made crescent rolls, the kind that came in a tube. Normally I would have been disappointed that I didn't get to pop the tube, but I was too tired and preoccupied to care.

I pushed the laptop to one side, planning to watch the earlier footage after eating. Vance hadn't passed by the reception desk when he left, but the camera might have caught him arriving that morning or earlier in the afternoon. I knew the odds were against me, but even if the odds were infinitesimal, they were better than zero. And I wasn't ready to give up.

"How's the stroganoff?" Bobbie asked.

I stared at my empty bowl. "It must have been good." I plucked another roll from the basket and slathered on so much butter it dripped onto my arm.

Bobbie handed me a napkin as I was about to lick it

off. "Maybe you should rest your eyes for a while. You look exhausted."

I yawned. "Can't." Kit's eyes peeked out from underneath the sofa. "Remember when Mom dropped her off at the beach house?"

Bobbie chuckled. "I remember how angry you were, but you know, sometimes Angela gets it right. She knew you needed someone, and Kit sure needed you."

At the sound of her name, Kit struggled to come out from under the sofa.

"She's put on weight since we got here. It didn't use to be such a tight fit for her to get under there." Feeling brave, I brought up another subject. "I saw her locket at the pawnshop in Bernard's building."

"Angela's?"

I shook my head. "Julia's. The one with the sapphire." I put my hand in my pocket and wrapped my hand around the locket, as if to make sure I hadn't dreamt of meeting with Isabella.

Bobbie's mouth dropped open, and she didn't even try to hide her shock. "Are you sure it's the same one?"

"Unless someone else put my baby picture in their locket, then yeah. It's hers."

"How did you recognize it?"

"It's in every picture I've ever seen of her." True, there weren't that many—maybe six or seven over the years—but I stared at each one until every detail was burned into my brain.

"I guess that means you were right." Bobbie's voice, barely more than a whisper, trembled. "She came here and didn't tell me."

"And me," I reminded her. "You'd think she'd want to meet me, but noooo. She couldn't be bothered."

"Why?" she asked, but she knew neither of us had the answer. We sat in silence, then she picked up our bowls and carried them into the kitchen.

I followed her. "There's something else. She's not the one who sold it to the pawn shop."

Bobbie stopped with the dishwasher half open. "Who did?"

I shrugged. "The guy at the pawnshop wouldn't tell me. Privacy regulations or something. It looked like the chain had broken, so she might have dropped it somewhere, and whoever found it sold it."

"Is it for sale? We can stop by first thing and get it."

I didn't want to tell her about meeting my aunt. "It's not there anymore. Someone already bought it."

She closed the dishwasher and took a deep breath, letting it out slowly. "You must have seen it the other day when we visited Mr. Fernsby's office. Why did you wait so long before telling me?"

That was a good question. "Maybe I wanted to have a secret of my own."

I didn't wait for her response. I grabbed the bag of cinnamon rolls and heated one up for a few seconds in the microwave.

"When I finish eating this, I'm going to get back to work." I sat down at the kitchen table, impatient to get back to work but not wanting to get the laptop sticky.

Bobbie nodded. "I'll put on a pot of coffee. I have a feeling you'll need it."

Bobbie nudged my elbow, and I jerked awake, lifting my head from the table.

"I fell asleep?" I rolled my stiff shoulders and glimpsed the sun peeking through the curtains. "Is it morning? Why did you let me sleep?"

She set a cup of coffee next to me. "You expected me to stay up all night to keep you awake? A good night's sleep enhances cognitive functioning, and I need all of that I can get at my age."

After a few sips of coffee and some more stretching, I glared at the laptop. "I watched the entire day starting at five AM until after the police came. Not a single glimpse of anyone who might have been Vance."

"What about the fake Mrs. Vance?"

I propped up my head with one hand. "We have no idea what she looks like without her disguise. I'd guess her between five-foot-six and eight, don't you think? I would have pegged her around 180 pounds, but under all those layers—" I made a quick calculation, "probably 140 or 150."

"Average height and slender or average build," Bobbie said. "I can see the problem."

"Yeah, that describes plenty of people. Even you or Gypsy."

"You would have recognized Gypsy, even in disguise."

"Would I?" I wondered. "I'm not sure. But I would have noticed if she had some sort of special interest in Kit, which she doesn't. Boy, now I'm starting to suspect your friends." I chuckled. "Maybe the fake Mrs. Vance was Henry in drag."

Bobbie shook her head. "He's too tall." She gestured to the laptop. "Could you tell how tall the dark-haired woman was?"

"Not really." I yawned and guzzled the last of my coffee, holding the still-warm cup in my hands. "You think she might have pretended to be Mrs. Vance? That would have been quite a disguise."

"She looks like she's in disguise in the video. All that makeup and hair. And the low-cut top that would assure that most men and some women wouldn't take a close look at her face."

"Hmmmm..." I pulled the laptop closer, found the timestamp on the video where I'd spotted the mystery woman, and took a screenshot. Transferring that to my phone, I stood and headed for the coat closet.

"Going somewhere?" Bobbie asked.

"Sugarbuns is open this time of the morning, aren't they?"

"Like any good bakery, they open at six." Bobbie raised one eyebrow. "But we still have a couple of cinnamon rolls left over from your last visit."

"I'm not going for cinnamon rolls. I'm going for information."

Chapter Nineteen

B obbie deemed the streets safe from ice and mud, so I laced up my running shoes. As I pulled my jacket on, Bobbie informed me that Vance's daughter Jan planned to come to Arrow Springs to pick up Kit at the assigned time.

The reality sunk in. "That doesn't give us much time, does it?"

I headed down the hill at a brisk jog. The street felt deserted at this early hour as I ran past closed shops and businesses. Arrow Springs Inn looked cozy from outside looking in, with the twinkling Christmas tree and colored lights in the window.

When I stepped inside Sugarbuns, at least a dozen people filled the small bakery. I breathed in the aroma of freshly brewed coffee and baked goods. Mitsy grinned when she saw me, but her smile quickly faded. "Where's Kit?"

"Sorry, just me this morning." Good thing, too. I

wasn't sure the other patrons would appreciate a dog in their favorite bakery, especially one that shed the way Kit did.

All I wanted was info, but I got in line, anyway. Might as well get a latte while I was here and maybe a warm chocolate croissant. When it was my turn, I ordered and waited for her to hand me my latte and pastry.

"You told me you never forget a face." I held up my phone with the screenshot of the dark-haired woman. "Have you seen this woman around lately?"

Mitsy leaned closer and tilted her head. I could almost see the gears turn inside her mind.

"This is going to sound crazy," she said. "But there was this older woman who came in a couple of days ago. Her facial structure is pretty much identical. Maybe they're related?"

"Can you describe her?" I asked.

The man behind me, tired of waiting, called out, "Can you two talk later? I'm going to be late for work."

"Shush," Mitsy said. "Everyone knows you retired six months ago, and your wife isn't in any hurry for you to get home." She turned back to me. "She wore a knit hat and no makeup. All she asked was where the police station was since she had the old address before they moved to Acorn Street."

"Thanks," I said. "You've been an enormous help."

She grinned. "I have? How?"

"I'll tell you later, I promise." Or maybe she'd read it on the news.

I strolled along the shops munching on my croissant, sipping my latte, and putting all the pieces together. It was the dark-haired woman who had put on a wig and pretended to be Mrs. Vance at the police station. She'd also been at the inn the day of the murder. Did she kill Guy Patro-whatsit?

Finding myself in front of the Arrow Springs Inn, I stood on the sidewalk, feeling exhilarated at solving one piece of the puzzle but frustrated at not knowing what to do next.

Should I go inside and see if there were any guests I hadn't yet talked to? Maybe Gary could tell me if any of the guests had been staying there since the day of the murder. But would he? I felt a little guilty using the stolen pinky ring to manipulate him, but if it helped me find a murderer, wasn't it worth it?

"Hi, Whit."

I swung around at the sound of Henry's voice. "Oh, hi."

"You look a little lost," he said. "Everything okay?" He paused. "Oh, sorry. Today's the day you have to give Kit back, isn't it?"

I nodded, not wanting to say it out loud. Besides, I still wanted to pretend it wasn't happening.

"Are you taking her back to Vance?" he asked. "It's a long drive to Riverside. Want me to go along?"

I shook my head. "His daughter is driving up here."

"Oh." He sounded as disappointed as I felt. "What time?"

"Our deadline is three PM." I glanced at my watch. "And I'm not giving her back a minute early."

"I don't blame you. That mutt's worth a lot," he said, adding, "to you, that is. I can tell how you feel about her."

That mutt's worth a lot... Someone else had used those same words. Someone recently... I searched my brain for the memory, but it seemed to slip out of my reach.

"Everything okay?" he asked. "You seem miles away."

"Oh sure." I gave him a meek smile. "It'll all work out in the end, I'm sure. I gotta get home. Guess I'll see you around."

"Sure." He looked as if he wanted to say something but changed his mind. "Let me know if there's anything I can do."

As I turned to walk away, the phrase went round and round in my mind until I finally remembered. When I'd gone to room 281 to see the man I'd thought was Jonathan Vance, there'd been another person in the room. They'd said, "That mutt is worth a lot."

And that person had murdered Guy Pavlakovich.

Chapter Twenty

Glancing back to make sure Henry wasn't watching, I took off at full speed for home. When I burst through the door, Kit scrambled out from under the sofa and began leaping into the air as if she hadn't seen me for days.

Bobbie appeared in the kitchen doorway. "What's got into you?"

"Henry," I gasped.

"Look, whatever you do as two consenting adults is fine, but I don't need to know the details."

"Henry has something to do with it." I struggled to catch my breath. "With Kit. Maybe with the murder."

"Calm down and come into the kitchen so I can take the cookies out of the oven before I burn the house down."

"You're baking cookies at a time like this? What are you thinking?"

She put her hands on her hips. "You stress eat. I stress bake. It's a very symbiotic relationship."

I could hardly argue with that. Kit followed me into the kitchen, prancing around my feet, not a care in the world. If she only knew.

I glanced at the wall clock ticking the minutes away. "We don't have much time."

She pulled a batch of sugar cookies from the oven. "We have five hours. Sit down and explain yourself."

How could I explain all the little things that added up to Henry not being the good guy he seemed to be? I ran them over in my mind while Bobbie poured me a cup of coffee.

I took a seat at the kitchen table and watched as Bobbie calmly transferred cookie stars, wreaths, and Christmas trees to a rack to cool.

"First," I began, "he was asking Mitsy at Sugarbuns about me."

Bobbie transferred a previous batch of cookies onto a plate and carried them to the table along with icing and sprinkles. Did she really expect me to decorate cookies at a time like this?

"That's not surprising. He's obviously interested in you." She set a Santa-shaped cookie on a plate in front of me, and Kit jumped up on my lap to grab it. I was too quick for her, pushing the plate out of her reach.

Instead of decorating the cookie, I broke it in two and shoved half in my mouth. "Would you ask a complete stranger about someone you're interested in?"

Bobbie took a seat across from me. "Probably not, come to think of it."

"Second, Kit went right up to him the first time she saw

him like she knew him. You know she doesn't like men." I let that sink in, but Bobbie didn't react. "And third, he knows Vance lives in Riverside. I don't remember telling him that."

"Someone else might have mentioned it."

"And fourth, he said..." I struggled to remember his exact words. "He said, 'that mutt is worth a lot,' or something close to that."

"She is worth a lot to you." She reached over to scratch Kit's ear and sweet talked to her. "You're worth your weight in gold, aren't you? Yes, you are!"

"When I went to see the fake Jonathan Vance, I heard a second person in room 281. Remember, I told you? I couldn't tell if it was a man or a woman, but I heard a few words: 'That mutt's worth a lot.' Almost the exact same words Henry said."

Bobbie considered what I'd said. "Could you tell if it was him? Was Henry the person you heard behind the door?"

"It must have been him. You and I know Kit is worth a lot, and not in a 'she's worth the world to me' kind of way. Have you ever wondered why she can jump twice as high as a normal dog? Or run for a mile, keeping up with me and hardly be panting?"

"What are you saying?"

I looked at the cute little fluffy six-pound dog in my lap, who tilted her head as if she had a question for me. "Hey, Kit. I'm the one with the questions here. What is your story? What did they do to you to give you superpowers?" Setting Kit on the ground, I returned my focus to Bobbie. "I think the vet would have told me if she had bionic limbs." I held up my index finger, wanting a moment to put the pieces together.

"What is it?"

Adrenaline surged inside me as a memory surfaced. "I ran into Henry one morning at the inn, the day I thought I saw Julia. That was the morning of the murder."

"Was he staying there?" she asked.

"No, he checked into the inn the day after the murder. He was there for breakfast, or maybe he was following me, but that's not the point."

"Then what is the point?"

"He plucked one of Kit's dog hairs off my jacket. And I don't remember him tossing it. I think he kept it."

Bobbie's eyebrows drew together. "Why in the world would he keep a dog hair?"

Only one reason I could imagine, and the more I thought about it, the more everything made sense. "For DNA testing."

Bobbie's eyebrows scrunched together as she tried to understand. "Like that advertisement to test your dog and see what breeds they are?"

"Yes, just like that. Only Henry wanted to know if Kit is the dog he's looking for."

My phone buzzed with a text from Tess. I groaned.

"I hope that's not bad news," Bobbie said. "I think we've had enough for quite a while."

I sighed. "Tess is driving home and wants to have lunch." I began typing a response, that start with, "Sorry, no can do."

Bobbie gently touched my arm. "You should go."

"You're kidding, right? Go have a leisurely lunch

while a murderer is on the loose and Vance's daughter is probably already on her way to take Kit from us forever?"

"No, of course not." Bobbie patted my hand, then carried our mugs to the sink. "Just drive into town and say goodbye. In the meantime, I'll call Bernard and see if there's something we can learn about Henry. Do you know his last name?"

"He never told me his full name." How could I get it? "I'll ask Gary. He's been much more cooperative since we didn't turn him into the cops for taking the pinky ring."

"Good thinking. Go see Tess and talk to Gary. Call me if you get the name and I'll get Bernard on it right away. He's probably still at the police station looking through traffic cam footage. Poor thing."

I returned Tess's text, and we agreed to meet in the inn's lobby in fifteen minutes. That would give me time to talk to Gary. I grabbed my jacket and keys and stepped outside. The clear, sunny skies of the previous day had given way to dark clouds. I hopped into my car for the short drive into town.

A parking spot right out front made me think my luck might have changed, but when I stepped inside the lobby, my hopes sank. Instead of Gary, the woman I'd met the day before stood behind the front desk. I sucked in a breath, ready to see if I could charm her out of the information I needed.

Before I made it halfway across the lobby, I heard Tess call my name. She strode down the stairs in jeans and a crisp white shirt, elegant and polished as always. She gave me air kisses.

"I'm glad you got here early," she said. "The weather

app says there's a huge snowstorm on the way, so I'm driving back early. I want to get down the mountain while I can. Why don't we get a quick bite in the dining room?"

I had too many things on my mind to sit and make small talk. "I'm not hungry."

"Coffee then, or a mimosa." She grinned. "Actually, a mimosa sounds great right now. Come on, who knows when I'll see you next?"

I gave in and followed her to the dining room. Tess ordered her mimosa, and I asked for iced tea. I knew we should be making small talk, but I struggled to focus or even pay attention to her words. In just a few hours, Jan would arrive to get Kit. If she'd looked at the weather report, she might even come early.

I refocused as she said, "... and he might come to L.A. to visit."

"Huh?" I blinked, completely lost. "Who?"

"Elijah," she said. "Who did you think I meant?" She prattled on, oblivious to my lack of interest. "Do you think Henry will come back to visit you? You two seemed pretty tight the other night."

"Mmm hmm." I wasn't sure how much to tell her, but I certainly wasn't going to share my suspicions about Henry. "Sorry, they're coming to get Kit in..." I checked the time on my phone. "Less than four hours. I'm having trouble focusing on anything else."

"I understand," Tess said, kindly. "You've really gotten attached to that little dog. I hope—"

The sound of a woman's voice, somewhat hysterical, came from the lobby. What was Bobbie doing here?

"Excuse me." I left Tess at the table and hurried to find out why she'd come to the inn.

Bobbie's mouth dropped open the moment she saw me. "Whitley!" She hurried over and grabbed me in a tight hug. She whispered in my ear. "You're okay."

I managed to say, "Can't breathe," and she released me. "Yes, of course I'm okay. Why wouldn't I be?"

Bobbie pursed her lips and gave her head. a little shake. "I got a call that said you'd been in a terrible accident. I don't understand. I thought they meant a car accident, but then I saw your car out front and—"

"What are you talking about?" I demanded. "Who called you?"

She blinked, and her eyes darted about, unfocused. "I... I don't know."

A sinking feeling came over me. "Where's Kit?"

"She's at home." Bobbie sounded defensive. "I didn't have time to wait for anyone to come watch her. I thought you were..." She didn't finish her sentence.

I muttered a few expletives, ran out of the lobby, and out the front door. Bobbie chased after me and reached the car just in time before I drove off without her.

"I'm sure Kit's fine," she said doubtfully as she buckled her seatbelt. Whether or not she was right, I had no way of knowing, but I was sure of one thing.

Kit wouldn't be there when we got home.

Chapter Twenty-One

Huge, wet snowflakes hit the windshield as I pulled into the driveway, tires squealing. Bobbie clutched the armrest as I slammed on the brakes and threw the car into park. Heart pounding, I leapt out of the car and raced to the door. Grasping the handle, I turned it. Unlocked. Not a good sign.

Inside, the house was silent and still. Calling out Kit's name, I dashed from room to room, only to return to the living room with a growing sense of dread when Bobbie entered.

"She's not here." I heard the desperation in my voice.

Bobbie kept her voice calm and controlled. "Did you check under the sofa?"

Dropping to the floor, I crawled on my hands and feet, but she wasn't there. Not willing to give up, I frantically searched under and behind every piece of furniture in the house. Bobbie rustled a bag of treats, calling, "Kit, come here Kit. I have a treat for you."

If the word "treat" hadn't lured Kit out, then I had to admit she wasn't there. I'd looked in every nook and cranny in the house.

"Wait." A wave of hope washed over me. "I put that tracker on her." I yanked my phone out of my pocket and homed in on Kit's location. "She's in the front yard!" I ran out the front door calling out her name. Bobbie appeared on the front porch while I homed in on the location the app indicated. Something shiny reflected from under the newly fallen snow. I knew what it was before I picked it up. Kit's collar.

I stood in the yard and announced, "She's been dognapped."

"No, no," Bobbie insisted. "She's just gotten out again."

Bobbie coaxed me back inside as I tried to make sense of my swirling thoughts. I collapsed onto the sofa, overwhelmed by a jumble of emotions. A knock on the door jarred me from my stupor. Flinging the door open, I found Tess on our doorstep.

I greeted her with, "Oh, it's you."

"That's a great way to talk to a friend." She stepped inside, not waiting for an invitation. "Especially one you just ran out on without saying goodbye."

"Sorry," I grumbled, not really caring what she thought at that moment.

"Kit is missing," Bobbie explained. "I'm sure she just got out again. She's done it plenty of times before."

"She's been dognapped." I took off my jacket and threw it on the sofa. For once, Bobbie didn't scold me. "And I know who took her."

"Who?" Tess asked.

"Henry." I waited for her to laugh at me, but she didn't.

She nodded thoughtfully. "I always thought there was something fishy about that guy. Did you ever notice how he had an answer for everything? 'My friend has a cabin up here; I can work from anywhere...' But he never really talked about himself, and he asked a lot of questions about you." Her eyes widened. "And Kit. He seemed really interested in her. What's up with that dog, anyway?"

I'd tell her, but all I had were theories, and at that moment, what I needed was action. "I need your help. I'm going to rescue Kit."

She grinned. "I'm in."

The roads were barely visible beneath a blanket of thick, white powder, and I backed the car out of the driveway carefully. The windshield wipers labored to clear away the heavy, wet snow. On the short drive back into town, I told Tess to call Henry at the inn.

"I have his cell number," she said. "I could text him."

I shook my head. "We need to know if he's in his room."

"You think he has Kit, don't you?"

I nodded, hoping beyond hope he wouldn't harm her.

The hotel operator transferred her to Henry's room, and relief washed over me when he answered. He hadn't left town yet.

Tess asked Henry to have lunch with her, but I could tell by her expression he'd turned her down. She wasn't about to give up that easily.

"I'm leaving town," she explained in a cooing voice. "I wanted to say goodbye before I left." Pause. "What if I stick around a bit longer? Maybe we could have dinner?"

She listened to his answer, then hung up.

"He's not going for it. Sorry, Whit."

"It's not your fault." I did my best to reassure her, despite my disappointment. "I doubt anyone could convince him to leave his room. What if Kit started barking and one of the guests complained?"

I parked the car on a side street and willed my brain to come up with a plan.

Tess, wanting to be helpful, suggested, "We could wait outside for him to leave. There's only two exits, one in front and one in back."

I shook my head. "That could take forever. And what if he's done something to Kit? Or plans to?"

Her eyes widened. "You think he'd hurt that sweet little dog? Who could do such a thing?"

"What happened to, 'she's just a dog'?"

She waved a hand in dismissal. "That's just me being tough and pretending I don't give a crap about anyone or anything. You need a tough exterior in this business. But the truth is, I have a soft, gooey center. Like you."

"Like me?" I stared at her, stunned. "You obviously don't know me at all. I'm tough as nails, right to the core."

"Uh-huh, sure," she said, skepticism in her voice. "That's why we're here in a snowstorm rescuing a tiny dog." She let that sink in for a moment. "What's the plan, then? You're as close to being a superhero as anyone I've ever met. How are you going to save the day?"

"I don't want to save the day," I said. "Just one little yippy dog."

◆ ➤

How much had Bobbie learned in her brief time as Bernard's apprentice? Might as well find out. I texted her, but instead of answering, she called me.

I got right to the point. "I need to know how to break into the Arrow Springs Inn. Like through one of the second-floor windows."

She didn't try to talk me out of it, and instead asked what sort of windows they had.

"The normal up and down kind." I had no idea what they were called.

"Oh, good," she said. "Sash windows are quite easy to pry open." She provided a quick tutorial, concluding with, "Or you can just break the glass, but that can be noisy."

I left instructions with Tess on what I needed her to do and got out of the car, pulling the hood of my jacket up. Opening the trunk, I was pleased that Bobbie had filled it with all the tools a good private investigator—or cat burglar—might need.

Luckily, I rarely cleaned all the junk out of my car, which meant a backpack I'd taken on a hike months earlier was still in there. I emptied the contents, replacing them with a screwdriver, flashlight, and crowbar.

I kept my steps slow and my gaze steady as I rounded the back of the Arrow Springs Inn. Scanning the empty streets, I realized I didn't need to worry about being noticed, since the weather meant few people lingered outdoors.

Tess had told me which room Henry was staying in, and I didn't bother asking her how she knew. Setting my phone on silent, I took a few steps back and checked out the back of the inn. From my brief time in the other room where I'd found the fake Vance's body, I remembered one large window in the bedroom and a smaller one in the bathroom. Counting three little windows and three big ones from the end, I identified Henry's room.

My phone vibrated with a text from Tess. *Ready when you are.*

Larger granite blocks along the corners of the building would provide decent footing, but if I went up that way, I'd have to make my way along a narrow ledge to his room.

Or I could start directly below his window and go straight up, but running my hands along the pebbly granite blocks, I gave up on that idea. The blocks fit tightly together without crevices for me to grab onto or slip a toe into. Looked like I'd be doing a ledge walk.

Going up was as easy as the rock wall at the gym, and minutes later, I reached the second story. I eyed the ledge with apprehension. I'd done plenty of stunts like this, but always with a harness. If I fell during a shoot, it would only hurt my pride. I liked to get stunts right the first time, but no one, not even me, was perfect. This time, I had to be perfect.

With a deep, calming breath, I slid one foot forward, knocking a rock off the ledge. I watched it fall to the ground and break into pieces on the concrete walk. If I had any sense, I'd turn back, but then what? I had no evidence to take to the police. And once Henry left town, I'd never see Kit again.

Taking another deep breath and holding it, I took the first tentative step. The ledge was wider than I'd first thought, and my confidence returned. Leaning against the wall, I crept one step at a time, feeling for each new foothold.

Snow blew onto the ledge, making the progress painfully slow. As I passed the first window, I leaned against the wall, shivering in the cold. "You can do this," I whispered to myself. "You have to do this."

Glancing downward, I knew I wasn't going back down that way. I turned my attention to all the things Kit, and what I would do once she was safe. First, a nice steaming cup of hot chocolate with extra marshmallows—the tiny ones. Kit couldn't have chocolate. She didn't know what she was missing.

I reached the next window and hope swelled in my chest. Kit and I would be together again soon. Slowly, I crept along the ledge past the next two windows. Finally, I reached what I hoped was Henry's bathroom window. I peered in at the white-tiled room, looking for signs of life, but all I saw was a toothbrush.

After what felt like an eternity, I reached Henry's window.

I carefully leaned around the window frame and peered inside. Henry's suitcase lay on the flowered bedspread next to a pet carrier. But where was he? Where was Kit? Henry came into view just as Kit's head popped up from the suitcase. The little traitor actually wagged her tail, but I sighed in relief at the sight of her.

Leaning back against the granite wall, I pulled out my phone and texted Tess with nearly numb fingers. *Now.* My heart pounded while I waited. I took another look through the window, watching and waiting.

Henry stopped packing, and Kit barked. I could almost hear Henry telling her to be quiet. He turned the TV on, then took Kit into the bathroom, returning without her. That was his mistake and my lucky break, or at least I hoped so. As quickly as I dared, I backtracked to the bathroom window. Kit wouldn't be happy about being locked in there.

I couldn't tell if the window was latched or not. Pressing my palms against the lower sash window, I tried to push it up, but it didn't budge.

Not knowing how much time I had, I pulled the crowbar from the backpack and slid the curved end between the bottom of the window frame and the sill. After making sure I was secure on the ledge, I twisted the crowbar and the window popped open.

I stuck my head in. Kit ran over to greet me, prancing and hopping around. I reached for her, but the window was too high up. "Jump, girl," I whispered. She lay down and rolled over.

Looked like I was going in. I pulled myself up and swung my leg over the windowsill, barely fitting through the small opening. I dropped to the floor as quietly as I could manage.

Pressing my ear against the door, I could hear Henry talking to Tess and the impatience in his muffled voice. I frantically went through all the possibilities of how to get out of the hotel alive with Kit.

Finally, I heard him say clearly, "Goodbye, Tess." The door slammed.

I stood behind the door and waited. When the door swung open, I pushed hard against it, shoving him back into the room. Not wasting any time, I emerged from the bathroom with Kit tucked under my left arm.

Henry stood between me and the door.

Chapter Twenty-Two

My heart raced and every muscle tensed while my eyes darted around the room for a weapon. Spotting a lamp on the nightstand, I lunged for it and brandished it like a club.

Henry held up his hands as if ready to surrender. "I'm not the enemy, Whit." He sounded so sincere I almost believed him. "I'm just trying to keep your dog safe."

"You dognapped Kit to keep her safe?" I couldn't believe he expected me to believe that. "From whom?"

"There's someone not nearly as nice as me who wants that dog, dead or alive."

"Liar!" I swung the lamp as hard as I could. He caught the lamp and grabbed my wrist, twisting it. I yelped in pain, dropping the lamp, but keeping hold of Kit.

He snarled. "You don't know what you're dealing with, little girl."

"I'm not a little girl." I gave his shin a sharp kick. He

groaned in pain, but his vise-like hold on my wrist only tightened as he twisted my arm around my back.

I stomped hard on his foot, and he threw me face down on the bed. "You like it rough, huh?"

Head butts were always a last resort, but I was out of options. I swung my head back with all my strength. The back of my skull connected with a thud, and he cried out. I ignored my pain and rolled over in time to see him clutching his face. I gave him a shove with both feet, sending him staggering back against the wall.

Racing to the door, I'd reached for the handle when Henry grabbed me by the hair and yanked me back into the room. He slammed my back against the wall as Kit yelped and flew from my arms.

"Too bad it had to end this way." He sounded almost regretful as his body pressed against me and his hands closed around my throat. "I was starting to like you." I clawed at his hands as I struggled to breathe.

"You—" I managed to get out a few words I would never have used in polite company.

"I don't want to hurt you, Whit," he said, his voice surprisingly gentle. "But I'm leaving with that dog, and you're not going to stop me."

My eyes focused on the blood pouring from his nose. If I didn't do something fast, I'd be another murder victim for everyone in town to talk about.

This was no time to play nice.

In one quick move, I mustered all my strength and jerked my knee up, aiming for his groin. As he moaned, doubled over in pain, I snatched up Kit and ran out the door. For the second time that week, I ran down the stairs of the Arrow Springs Inn and out the front door. This time, I ran to save Kit instead of chasing after her.

The snow came down in wet clumps, not at all what the Hallmark Channel had led me to expect. Could I drive in this mess? I turned the corner where my car sat covered in a heavy blanket of thick, wet snow.

With no idea how long before Henry would burst through that door and chase after us, I ran into the empty street.

A man's voice called my name from behind me. Henry. Now that he'd seen me, it was too late to duck into the bakery, and the police station was blocks away. Could I make it before he caught up with me?

A sudden roar came from down the street, growing louder, and I froze as it came straight at me. The snowmobile came to a stop. I didn't recognize the driver bundled up against the elements.

"Hop on," a woman's voice called over the sound of the engine.

With Henry behind me, I didn't think twice and jumped onto the back, tucking Kit under my jacket. I held on as tightly as I could as we sped away out of town. Minutes later, we pulled up in front of Rosa's house.

Rosa and I climbed off the snowmobile. "What about Bobbie?" I called after her as she headed to the front door. "She might be in danger. Henry knows where I live."

"You text her and let her know I'm on the way." She unlocked the front door and waved me inside. "Start up a pot of coffee. I'll get her and come right back."

Shaking off the snow, I stepped into her modestly furnished living room. I took off my boots and let Kit out from under my jacket. She ran around the room, sniffing every corner before jumping onto the sofa and rubbing her body on a quilt draped over the back.

I sent Bobbie a text: *Rosa coming to get you. Will explain later.*

After hanging up my coat, I made my way to the kitchen and found a jar of ground coffee. As it brewed, I stood by the front window, peeking out through the lace curtains. There was no way Henry could have gotten to Bobbie's place before Rosa—not with the way the snow had been coming down for the past few hours.

Kit rubbed against my stocking feet.

"You worried too?" I took a seat on the sofa, and she jumped on my lap. "She'll be fine. No need to worry."

But I had plenty to worry about. Jan would be on her way to come get Kit by now. Would she be able to make it in this weather? The thought gave me a moment of hope until I remembered that big truck of theirs wouldn't have a problem getting up the hill in the storm.

My phone buzzed with a message from Bobbie. *Come home. We're waiting for you.*

How odd. She always preferred to call. Besides, did she expect me to walk home in this weather? It wasn't more than a couple of blocks, but still...

My reply said: *Send Rosa to pick me up?*

No answer.

I called Bobbie, but it went straight to voicemail. Staring at the phone screen, trying to decide what to do, I read the time: Jan would arrive within the hour.

Finally, a response came from Bobbie's phone. *Snow-mobile out of gas. Come home and bring Kit.*

Something felt off. A lot of things, actually. The possibilities ran through my mind, and one thought sent a chill down my spine—Was Henry holding Bobbie and Rosa captive?

I didn't know how he would have made it to Bobbie's house so quickly, but I had to go find out. If there was any way I was being lured into a trap, I wasn't bringing Kit with me.

"You stay here," I warned Kit as I turned off the coffeepot and pulled my jacket on. "Be a good girl, okay?"

She followed me to the door, obviously intending to come with me.

"Look, it's too cold outside, okay?"

She cocked her head to one side as if to say, "Then carry me in your jacket again."

"It's not safe." I sighed. "Why am I having a conversation with you? You have no idea what I'm saying. I'll be back as soon as I can, okay?"

Somehow, I slipped out the front door without letting her out. I trudged through the heavy snow, hoping all my fears were unfounded and Bobbie would be waiting with a warm cup of hot cocoa with extra marshmallows. I kept that thought in mind while the wet snow seeped into my jeans from the knees down and my toes grew numb.

When I arrived at the house, I circled around the back to the kitchen window, half expecting to see Henry had tied up Bobbie and Rosa. I peeked in, both relieved and disappointed to see my grandmother and her friend sitting at the kitchen table with Jan. No wonder Bobbie had said to bring Kit—Jan had arrived early.

My heart fell into my cold, wet feet. I figured I might

197

as well go in, get warm, and let everyone know about the recent developments.

And then I heard a high-pitched bark.

Seriously? "How'd you get out?" I scooped up the wet, shivering dog and tucked her under my jacket. "Never mind. I don't even know why I asked. Let's go on in and get you dry and warm."

I took another look through the window and felt a soft growl vibrate through Kit's body.

"What's wrong, girl? Don't you like Jan?"

She squirmed in my arms as if trying to get free, and then she froze. Her ears perked up, and she began growling again.

"Shhh." I needed to think. If Kit hated Jan so much she'd growl at her through the window, how could I let her take our little dog from us—from me?

I leaned against the side of the house. What did we really know about Vance's daughter?

Jan didn't especially like dogs or care about the business. The business was about to go under, I guessed, since where could Vance house all those dogs if his house was foreclosed on? Bobbie had made a generous offer to Vance to let us keep Kit and hinted that she'd be willing to offer more.

Then why had Jan driven to Arrow Springs to pick up Kit?

What made the little mutt so special—so valuable— that both Henry and Jan would go to such lengths to gain possession of her?

I leaned in for another look at Jan. When we'd met her at her father's house, I'd barely got a glimpse of her. Luckily, the sun had dipped below the mountains, which I hoped meant she couldn't see me from where she sat in the brightly lit kitchen.

Peeking through the sheer curtains, I took a long look at her, imagining her with a wig and knit cap. She had the same high cheekbones as the dark-haired woman with all the makeup and the low-cut blouse who'd been in the hotel at the time of the murder.

Mitsy had connected the dark-haired woman and the lady who'd pretended to be Mrs. Vance. And now, watching Jan through the window, I knew she'd been the one behind both disguises. Did that mean she was the one who killed Guy Pavlakovich? Not Henry?

Before I could decide what to do, Jan stood and took a step away from the table. What I saw chilled me to the bone. She had a gun pointed right at Bobbie.

Chapter Twenty-Three

N ow what was I supposed to do? Call the police? They'd come barreling in no doubt, creating a potential hostage situation. I couldn't risk Bobbie or Rosa getting caught in any crossfire.

I felt in my pocket and pulled out the pen Kelvin had given me. Calling him to come rescue us seemed like the wrong move at a time like this, and I wouldn't forgive myself if he got hurt coming to rescue me.

"I'm not a damsel in distress, Kelvin." I whispered. "I think we should make that perfectly clear."

After taking a deep breath, I pressed the button.

Shoving it back in my pocket, I slogged through the snow around the side of the house until I reached the front door and pushed it open. Before I could stop her, Kit wriggled free and ran into the kitchen.

Taking off my soaked shoes, I followed her, hoping Jan might let me have a warm beverage before she shot me.

Jan, Rosa, and Bobbie sat at the table, almost looking like three friends sharing a pot of coffee.

Kit froze in place, growling, her teeth bared. Jan's gun now pointed at me.

"Is that really necessary?" I asked.

She gave me a wry smile. "It's insurance. I don't have any time to waste, and I need to get back down that mountain before they close the roads. The way the snow's coming down, that won't be long." She stood. "I'll take the dog."

"Let me at least dry her off." I grabbed a dish towel and crouched down, rubbing Kit vigorously as she tried to bite the towel.

"No time for that. Give her to me."

I kept rubbing Kit down while furiously trying to think of a way out of our dilemma. "She's shivering."

She lifted her gun, pointing it at my head. "Give her to me. Now."

I hesitated, and a chilling smile played on her lips. She slowly moved her arm, pointing the gun at Bobbie instead.

Bobbie didn't flinch, but Rosa gasped. "No! Don't shoot her, please!"

I picked up Kit and held her out to Jan. Kit growled, her teeth exposed.

"Hand me that towel," Jan demanded.

She wrapped Kit's head in the towel, then took the dog from me, holding her by the scruff. Kit wriggled like a wild animal. Jan kept her aim on Bobbie, but struggled to hold on to Kit, who kicked her way out of Jan's grasp.

Jan yelled, "You little—" as Kit ran out of the kitchen into the living room.

I could picture the little rascal in her safe space under the sofa. Jan glared at me, then her gaze softened. She took a seat at the kitchen table, the gun still pointed at my grandmother.

"I'll give you three minutes to get the dog and put her in a carrier or suitcase or whatever you have. Three minutes, starting now."

I always thought I was good in a crisis, but I couldn't think of what to do.

Bobbie must have recognized my state of paralysis. "The carrier is in the cabinet in the laundry room where I keep her food."

"Don't try to pull anything," Jan said. "In case you have any doubts, I *will* use this gun."

Quickly retrieving the carrier and Kit's treats, I handed Bobbie the carrier and called out to Kit. As I shook the bag, I called out, "Treats, Kit. I've got treats," but she didn't budge from her hiding place. I kneeled and peeked under the sofa. Big brown eyes stared back at me.

"It's okay, girl," I cooed. "Want a treat?"

Jan's voice called out from the kitchen. "Two minutes."

"Please, baby girl?" I felt my heart breaking. This little dog did nothing wrong, and in return, she'd been treated like a lab animal. Who knew what she'd been through in her brief life? I set a treat down a few inches from her nose.

Kit snatched the treat and then another, inching closer. If I tried to grab her too soon, she'd retreat under the sofa, so I held my breath, waiting for the right moment.

"One minute."

I stood and took a step back, ready to betray the one creature who'd always shown me love and loyalty.

I tapped my hands against my chest. "Alley-oop!"

Kit leapt into my arms, and I clutched her close, never wanting to let her go. I carried her to the kitchen where the carrier sat open on the kitchen table. Holding my breath, I shoved Kit inside and zipped it closed.

The sound of her whimper stole something from me, something I didn't even know I had. If I ever found myself alone with Jan in the future, I would not be responsible for what I did to her.

Jan stood and slung the carrier over her shoulder. The four of us froze at the sound of the front door opening. I glanced at Bobbie, who shrugged. Rosa's eyes were wide as saucers.

"Who is that?" Jan hissed.

"No idea."

My heart seemed to stop beating as Bobbie called out, "Hello, who's there?"

Henry appeared in the doorway, his hair wet and disheveled. "Oh, hello everyone," he said casually, as if I hadn't just beat the crap out of him. Blood crusted on his upper lip. "Having a tea party? Why wasn't I invited?"

"Who are you?" Jan asked.

He smirked. "I'm Henry. No need to introduce yourself, since, you see, I know exactly who you are, Jan. Tell me. Who was the highest bidder? Russia? China? Or maybe another corporation wanting to know how far our DNA technologies have come?"

"I'm leaving." Jan made a move to push past him, the carrier over her shoulder.

Henry grabbed her by the arm. "I don't think so."

Jan aimed her gun at Henry's chest and the two of them locked eyes.

"I was right," I said, not particularly caring at that moment if Jan shot Henry. "Kit is the product of genetic engineering."

Henry nodded, not taking his eyes off Jan. "The goal of our research is to find treatments and cures for diseases such as Parkinson's or muscular dystrophy."

"Ha!" Jan practically spit in his face. "Your company's goal is to make money. Curing diseases is chump change. How much would someone pay to be stronger and smarter? Or, better yet, make their kids smarter? People will pay huge bribes to get their average kids into a top university. What if they could just make brilliant babies?"

"That's not in the plans," Henry said, his voice even.

Jan sneered at him and raised her gun from his chest to his forehead.

"Go ahead, shoot me," Henry said. "My life is worth about two cents if that dog gets into the wrong hands."

"Why is that, Henry?" I asked, half out of curiosity and half to buy time.

"The experiments my company did weren't *entirely* legal. My team was hand picked by the company founder and instructed to maintain absolutely no records on site that would get the company in hot water. The board knew nothing. That dog was bred and raised in the lab. I used to come visit her and play with her, which worked out well in the long run, though I'm surprised you weren't suspicious of how she took to me so quickly."

"I was," I admitted. "But I trusted you. That was my

big mistake—trusting a murderer."

"I didn't kill anyone." Henry scowled and turned his gaze from me to Jan. "Guy Pavlakovich was Jan's partner. I'm guessing he tried to double cross her, and she repaid him with a knife to the throat."

Jan's expression didn't change. "When my dad told me he'd been hired to train Roxy, I knew right away something was up. She's not a normal dog. Then Guy showed up and said we could get a lot of money for her—I mean a *lot* of money. I jumped at the chance to get out of the dog training business. If I never see another stupid dog the rest of my life, it will be too soon."

"Now what?" Henry seemed way too blasé considering the situation, but maybe it was a coping mechanism and he was as freaked out as the rest of us.

"I've killed one person," she said. "What's one more? Your death won't stop me, so there's no need to be a martyr, Henry."

I held my breath, waiting to see what Henry would do, and the world seemed to stand still. I was pretty pissed off at Henry, but now that I knew he wasn't a murderer, I didn't want him shot point blank in our living room.

"Fine." Henry raised his hands and took a step backwards. "I can tell when I'm beat."

Jan backed out of the room until she reached the front door. "Anyone who follows me gets a bullet."

The moment the door closed behind her, I dashed into the kitchen, jerking open the junk drawer. Grabbing the shuriken, I ran for the front door.

"Don't!" Bobbie called after me. "She'll shoot you."

Stepping out onto the front porch, I spotted Jan nearly

at her truck.

She turned back and pointed the gun at me. "I'm an excellent shot. Do you really want to die today?"

Before I could answer, I heard a whirring sound in the distance. As it grew louder, I turned to see something in the air, something coming right for us.

A drone, about two feet wide, bobbed and weaved as it approached.

Jan walked backwards toward the truck, keeping her gun trained on me. The drone came closer and appeared to give me a little nod.

I jerked my head toward Jan, not sure how much the drone pilot could see. The drone hovered, turning right and then left, then began closing in on Jan.

"I will shoot you," Jan shouted as she fumbled with the driver's door. As the drone came closer, she seemed unsure of who or what she should shoot. It hovered, buzzing gently, then began circling her like an oversized gnat.

"Get away from me!" She pointed the gun at the drone and pulled the trigger.

I clutched the shuriken and pulled my arm back, knowing I only had one chance. As it flew through the air, several shots rang out. Jan must have heard the whistling sound because she turned and the five-pointed star hit her in the forehead.

With a scream, she fell to the ground next to the truck, and I rushed to her side. I put one foot on the gun as I opened the carrier. Kit hopped out, wagging her tail.

"I've got some good news for you, Jan," I said as she lay moaning and clutching her forehead. "You're not likely to see another dog for the next twenty-five years to life."

Chapter Twenty-Four

The next hour was a blur, with four police cars arriving at the same time as the ambulance.

Jan yelled at anyone who would hear her. "She attacked me! You should arrest her! I'm seriously injured!"

I pointed out the gun to one of the detectives who bagged it.

The paramedics bandaged Jan's forehead, but insisted on taking her to the emergency room to be checked out. Two officers helped handcuff her and put her on a gurney so she could be wheeled into the back of the ambulance.

Bobbie and Rosa flanked Henry, not giving him a chance to slip away.

"You need to arrest him, too," I told Deputy Wallenthorp, pointing at Henry. "He's a dognapper, and who knows what else."

Wallenthorp gave Henry a once-over, then turned

back to me. "I thought the woman we arrested was trying to steal your dog."

"She was," I said.

"At gunpoint," Bobbie added.

"And you think she killed Pavlakovich over the dog." He paused. "And this guy tried to steal the dog, too?"

"He didn't try," I explained. "He did steal her. I had to break into his room at the inn to get her back."

Wallenthorp gave me a long look, as he seemed to decide whether to ask me for more details about my daring feat. "What's so special about this dog?"

I glanced over at Henry, who shook his head. He didn't want the truth coming out about Kit being genetically modified, but did I?

All I wanted was to keep Kit safe.

"She's an exceptionally well-trained and talented performing dog," I explained, staying in the general vicinity of the truth. "She would be worth a lot to someone like Vance, although I'm not sure he had anything to do with his daughter's actions."

"Deputy Wallenthorp," Bobbie smiled kindly. "Why don't we go inside, and we can tell you everything over a nice cup of coffee and some cookies?"

Wallenthorp harrumphed. "Yes, that sounds like a good idea. I've got a lot of questions that need answering."

"So do I," Bobbie said as she led the way inside.

Henry held back, and I kept a close eye on him.

"You're not going anywhere, buddy." I gestured for him to follow the others.

"Can we make a deal?" he asked.

"A deal?" I felt Kit wag her tail against my side, and I

remembered that Henry had been kind to Kit when she was caged in a lab.

Rosa hovered nearby, holding her bulging purse close to her chest.

"I've got this," I assured her.

She pursed her lips, not convinced. She dug through her handbag and brought out what looked like a plastic gun. "Taser?" she asked, as if offering me a breath mint.

"I don't think that will be necessary." For some reason, I didn't expect Henry to try to harm me or escape. Not that I trusted him, but now that he'd seen me in action, he knew I could take him. I almost hoped he would give me an excuse to beat him up again.

Rosa scowled at Henry, then dug around again and pulled out a canister of pepper spray, pressing it into my hand. "You can never be too safe."

"Thanks, Rosa."

Henry and I waited for Rosa to go inside, then I crossed my arms and gave him a don't-mess-with-me look.

He cleared his throat. "If my involvement in this, um, incident, gets out, my career is over."

"You think I care... why?"

He gave me a pathetic look. "And if the truth about your dog's capabilities becomes public, my life may be in danger."

"Oh, poor you," I said humorlessly. "That's a little dramatic, don't you think?"

The look on his face told me otherwise. "If you want to keep that dog safe, you don't want anyone finding out you've got her." He paused while I considered the ramifications of his words. "If you agree not to press charges, I'll tell my boss that I wasn't able to locate the dog, and that I think she's dead."

Kit whimpered as if she knew what Henry had said, while I donned my best poker face.

"Why did you wait so long to steal Kit? You even spent the night on my sofa with Kit curled up next to you. You could have sneaked out in the middle of the night."

"That was the plan," Henry said. "I almost had her lured out of the door, but when I picked her up, she bit me and hid under the sofa. I didn't even realize she'd come out from her hiding spot until you woke me up the next morning."

"She bit you?" I grinned, thinking I'd give Kit extra treats later.

"She's incredibly loyal to you. Look," he continued. "If you pursue this, the worst I'll get charged with is dognapping. How long do you think I'll spend in jail? At the most, weeks. I might get off with thirty days of community service."

He was probably right. And any publicity around the case would likely give away Kit's identity and location to Henry's boss and anyone else who might be interested in a genetically superior dog. I sure didn't want that to happen.

"How do I know you'll keep your part of the bargain? And how do I know there's not another Jan or Pavlo-what's-his-name out there lurking who's going to come after her?"

He gave me a sincere smile and said, "I give you my word."

"Hah!" I didn't trust him or his word for a second. "Tell you what. You write up and sign a confession about the experiments you and your company are doing. I'll hold on to it for insurance—if you keep your side of the bargain, no one will ever see it."

"You're crazy." His eyebrows drew together tightly. "Why would I give you a signed confession?"

I grabbed him by the arm and tugged him toward the front door, calling out, "Deputy Wallenthorp!"

Henry yanked his arm away. "Give me a sec, okay?" He rubbed his arm where I'd squeezed it. It wasn't my fault I didn't know my own strength.

In a sing-song voice, I said, "I'm waiting..."

Henry had given up the nice-guy persona as he glared at me. "Fine. It's not like I have a choice. But if that document sees the light of day, then I will let my boss know exactly where they can find Kit. And, just so you know, I was told to bring her back dead or alive. I preferred alive, but the next person they send may not care."

"Creep." I gestured inside. "Let's get it over with."

Chapter Twenty-Five

The next morning, Bobbie asked me to go into town with her. "And bring Kit." She carried a large tote bag, and I had a pretty good idea what was in it.

Stepping out into an otherworldly scene, I squinted at the bright sun reflecting against the snow. The air, still with a peaceful hush, seemed to muffle every sound other than the rustling of the pine trees in the soft breeze. Their branches strained under the weight of the heavy snow. A few fluffy clouds floated by in an otherwise clear blue sky.

Once I'd gone back inside for my sunglasses, I trudged through the snow to my car, which sat under a good six inches of snow. The roads had been plowed, but unfortunately, no one had cleared the driveway.

"Who's going to shovel the driveway so I can get the car out?" I asked.

She smiled sweetly. "Nothing for you to worry about

right now. It's such a lovely day, why don't we walk? I could use a little exercise."

"Sounds good to me, but I'll warn you, it's slow going when Kit is along."

"I'm okay with a slow pace. It gives us a chance to enjoy the beautiful scenery." She waved her arm at the snow-covered landscape surrounding us. "How lucky are we to live in such a beautiful world? It's heavenly, don't you think?"

"Heavenly?" I thought that over as we made our way down the road. "Yes, now that Jan is in jail and Vance has agreed to let us keep Kit—"

"And you have that signed confession from Henry," she added.

I grinned. "He really hated doing that. I think that was the best part of all, making him suffer."

Nearly half an hour later, we finally made it to town. After stopping in at Sugarbuns for cinnamon rolls and lattes, we made our way to Security Plus to see Kelvin.

"Do you think Kelvin is building a robot army?" I asked Bobbie, who gave me a funny look.

"Why would you ask such a thing?"

I shrugged. "I'm just a curious sort of person, that's all."

Bobbie pushed the shop's door open, and I followed, tugging at Kit's leash to encourage her to keep up.

Kelvin emerged from the back room and stood behind the back counter. "Good morning, Mrs. Leland, how nice to see you. Nice to see you too, Whitley. What can I do for you today? Are you here to pick up more surveillance equipment?"

Bobbie approached him, carrying her tote bag. "We're here to offer our thanks."

He raised his eyebrows. "For what?"

Bobbie gave him an indulgent smile. "We'd also like to reimburse you for your loss." She set the bag on the countertop and pulled out the ruined drone. "I'm guessing it's beyond repair."

"What happened to your drone?" he said innocently. "It looks like it's been shot. Several times." He turned it over. "Yes, I'm afraid it's unrepairable."

"Oh," I said, leaning one elbow on the counter. "So that's how we're going to play it, huh? Plausible deniability?"

He grinned and gave me a wink. "How'd I do?"

I gave him a thumbs up. While Bobbie tried to offer him money for the drone and he did his best to refuse it, I wandered around the shop.

Kit tugged at the leash, eager to sniff every corner of the shop. After getting bored by the equipment and other items I knew nothing about, I peeked through the blinds at the bookshop across the street.

As I peered into the bookshop across the street, a face appeared in the window, and I jumped back in surprise. "Who was that?"

"Who do you mean?" Bobbie asked as Kelvin hurried over to my side.

Kelvin asked with widened eyes, "Was it a woman with a tanned face and spiky blonde hair?"

"Yes..."

"That is my nemesis."

Epilogue

As a black limousine pulled up beside me, the rear window rolled down, reminding me of a scene from a mafia movie. Isabella's face appeared.

"Hello, Isabella. Or should I say Aunt Isabella." That was a mouthful. "Or Aunt Izzy?"

"Please do not call me that." Her voice, as smooth and sweet as Sugarbuns' cinnamon rolls, held an edge. "Why don't you hop in the car, and we can talk privately."

"Talk?" I didn't trust this woman even if she was related to me.

"Yes, I'm headed for the airport. We can talk on the way and my driver can take you back. I can tell you all about your father if you'd like. You must be curious."

"I'm kinda busy." That's what I always told people when I didn't want to do something. It was an excuse that worked for all sorts of situations and people.

"Why are you so suspicious?" She laughed. "Do you think I'm going to harm you?"

Why did even talking to her make me feel unsafe? I could take care of myself, after all. Puny, little Isabella wasn't anyone I needed to worry about—not physically at least. But my instincts were telling me something wasn't right.

I hesitated. "Okay, I'll drive with you to the airport, but no funny business."

"No funny business? You say the funniest things, Whitley."

I narrowed my eyes. "Fine, I'll see you later." I took a few steps away from the car.

"Wait," she called after me. "No funny business."

I turned around, not sure if I should trust her. "Promise?"

She smiled, showing off dazzling white teeth. "I promise."

THANK YOU for reading *Hair of the Dog, an Arrow Investigations Humorous, Action-Adventure Mystery!*

To learn about Arrow Investigations next case involving Kit's former owner, look for **Triple Shot**—coming in fall 2023!

If you haven't yet read the Arrow Investigations prequel, *The Black Daiquiri*, you can download it when you sign up for updates at www.kcwalkerauthor.com.

KC Walker also writes and publishes sweet cozy mysteries under the name Karen Sue Walker. You can find her Bridal Shop Mysteries and Haunted Tearoom Mysteries on Amazon. Visit karensuewalker.com/books to learn more.

By the way, I love hearing from readers—you can email me at kc@karensuewalker.com.

Made in United States
North Haven, CT
15 August 2023

40326828R00133